TWELVE SUSPECTS

Michael A. Susko

AllrOneofUs Publishing
Baltimore, Md & Huntsville, Al

TWELVE SUSPECTS

First edition. August 6, 2021.

ISBN: 979-8223468011

Written by Michael A. Susko.

To lovers of history and mystery.

CHAPTER I

THE ORACLE

The emperor, Constantine, ordered the archives scoured for tales of the twelve who followed the sign, after he had seen a vision on the battlefield. Brief references in official histories were found, mostly condemning the movement as "the scourge of the human race," a "secret burial clan" or a "mystery cult" that drew from the "dregs of humanity." However, useful items surfaced that verified sites for building churches, monuments, and martyriums. It was critical for all such building projects that a physical relic to be found, especially from the original twelve.

In the course of the search, nothing was left unturned––from the libraries of Alexandria to the catacombs of limestone tufa under Rome. It was in the catacombs that a lengthy document was found by an aged *fossores*, a professional grave digger, who could recall the burials of early Christians lost to memory. The fossores along with an aged librarian had come directly to Constantinople by order of the emperor, as he held it of utmost importance to authenticate this report. The librarian, versed in Latin and Greek and who had already read the document, began his report.

"This document bears directly on your concern," he said, "written in first century script."

The emperor, rigidly posed on his throne as if an icon, leaned forward intently. "How was it found?" he asked the fossores.

"I was in the grave of a poor Christian. I was tired from a hard day of digging, and it was cool below. I went into an old section that I hadn't been since a child and checked for a grave of one in my family. But my memory failed me. They were all filled with bones. In one, a skeletal hand clasped a long lead tube."

"You stole from the hand of the dead?" enquired the emperor's theologian with displeasure.

"No," said the fossores. "It is with approval of the Priest of the diocese that I may take them, and for a small fee, he keeps them."

"He asked me to open the tube," said Minas, the librarian, "from which we found this papyrus rolled within."

"Whose tomb was it?" asked Eusebius, the emperor's theologian.

"We do not know. But he had an unusual ring," reported the fossores, handing it to the theologian.

"The seal of Tiberius," said Eusebius. "It looks authentic, but proof may be in the telling."

"A full reading is in order," said the emperor, becoming more relaxed in his bearing. He ordered the court to be dismissed, keeping the queen on his left, who held an equal appearance in majesty. Eusebius, the emperor's historian, sat on his right, and he could attest to the authenticity of the document and its orthodoxy.

"The report," Minas went on, "appears to be written by an imperial investigator. We do not have the very first part, nor the very last. The first crumbled upon opening and the last had been torn away. Thus, we don't know the name of the actual investigator, who avoided using his own name, although the beginning was certainly prefixed by it. We don't know the answer to the mystery either, though we may surmise one based on what we have."

"Read on then," said Constantine, showing a bit of impatience.

"One more thing needs to be said," said the librarian. "Fortunately, the document includes the oracle around which the story is centered."

"The superstitious bane of ancient Rome," said Eusebius, "but it may show the document's authenticity."

"I will translate the archaic words into more contemporary language," said the librarian.

"...disturbed by an oracle reported by the seer of the pontifical college, originally from Delphi, 130 years from the founding." The oracle reads:

From the bones of twelve,
A Phoenix shall rise that will rule Rome!

"The document continues with the words of the emperor at the time, and his reaction to the oracle over two hundred years ago."

"Read on," directed Constantine.

The librarian, who remained standing, cleared his throat, raised the scroll, and spoke:

"Bones!" the emperor exclaimed. "How can bones conquer Rome?"

The seer had said all he knew. "One cannot always explain the Gods," he offered, "but we could ask for another."

"No more!" shouted the emperor. "Lest it becomes worse. I can deal with bones."

The emperor entrusted me to find the meaning of the riddle, as I was an *amicus* of the throne, and had parried more than one assassination attempt. I agreed to his request and refrained from correcting the emperor. The oracle had not said that bones would rule Rome, but the *Phoenix*. Personally, I did not take stock in oracles, the ravings of the crazed priestesses in Delphi, sitting on ash pots of bones and breathing vapors from the earth. Still, intelligence filtered in from unlikely sources. By all appearances, the reference was to a new mystery cult, and I asked leave to find a companion expert on the matter, which he granted.

The emperor did not give much time. Within the week I was due and returned with a report. "No Sybil's book or priest in Rome cast further light on the matter, other than to say the Phoenix will rise from the east. There is a current prophecy there that a new master will one day arise."

"But twelve?" asked the emperor. "That is the key. It's a conspiracy of twelve."

"Sizes of conspiratorial groups can be different numbers," I said. "The number twelve suggests mystical connections."

The emperor angered. "Is that all we know? Just mystical mumbo jumble from the East!"

I kept my calm and continued my report. "There is more... The cult started in Jerusalem from which you have just returned. My informants tell me——"

"Jerusalem!" screamed the emperor, rising from his throne. "I will hear no more of her. I have just razed her!"

The emperor's outburst should have stopped me, but I ventured a bold comment. "The Phoenix, as we know, rises from ashes."

"Jerusalem is but crumbling blocks of stone! Nothing more will ever rise from her," the emperor ranted. "Nothing! She's littered with bones!"

"Bones ... the oracle," I reminded. This sobered the emperor. "Someone of David's Royal line may have survived in an outer area."

"A liquidation has been ordered. I am assured they will be thorough."

"Perhaps one or two have already escaped and went on to Alexandria or Tyre."

The emperor, however, barely heard me, caught up in his own reflection. "We are taking the oracle all wrong," he said. "There are 12 tribes of the Jews, and the Phoenix is the Roman nation, meaning the Roman eagle will rise victorious! That is the answer to your riddle!"

With that, the matter was suddenly dismissed, and the emperor refused to have the matter mentioned again. I was relieved of a rather tedious enterprise based on very little information.

Within two weeks, however, the emperor ordered me back into his presence. He had received recent intelligence that appeared to confirm the oracle. Before him stood an informant with a most unreliable look.

"Galileans!" he cried. "Stirring trouble again. This man said that they cast lots and divided the world among themselves."

"Prophetic lots," said the informant.

"How many of them?" I asked.

"Twelve," he answered.

"Twelve against the legions of Rome. Why should we fear them?"

But clearly the emperor was disturbed. If it had been ten, a 100, or even a thousand, it would not have bothered him. But *twelve*, the number of the oracle, its paltry size, and the impossibility of it, raised his ire.

"Divided the entire world, did they!" mocked the emperor. "And perform the twelve labors of Hercules?"

"There are women too," said the informant.

"I don't want to hear about women!" exclaimed the emperor, losing his temper. "What manner of men are they?"

"They are common men, fishermen, field laborers ... a few skilled tradesmen."

"Perhaps they hope to catch whales now," jested the emperor.

"One has already come to Rome," went on the informant.

"The conspiracy is already here?" questioned the emperor, his face becoming strained. "Yes, not long ago, Rome herself lay in ashes. So, the phoenix would rise here? These twelve must be sought out and killed!"

"But the oracle says the *bones* of twelve will rule," I dared to correct. "To kill them would only hasten the Phoenix's birth."

"Yes," said the emperor, bemused. "That is the trouble with oracles. They always mean something you do not expect. Or is that part of the plot? First, you must go to Delphi's oracle and find how bones should be fought."

"The informant says one of the twelve is already here."

"Then find him first. Go!" And with that, I was dismissed.

CHAPTER II

THE GEMONIUM

Philo had been my contact for years regarding mystery cults, helping me to determine if they were a threat against the Roman state. He had survived the service of many emperors and preferring to remain anonymous. He was simply referred to as the *Source*. He was indeed an excellent source, for he could become obsessed with esoteric things and access the most sensitive material. Yet he could also be detached and give an objective report. He had been initiated into several mystery cults and knew things that weren't found in any writings. He could tell critical things that an investigator would need to know and in a timely way.

This reminds me that I never saw him write things down, but he trusted everything to his phenomenal memory. No doubt this aided in not having him been detected by others. We hardly knew who he was, and Philo, as such, was simply the name used for this mission.

When Philo told the tales of the Mithra beast, lion-headed and snake entwined, or the maenads who in frenzy tore animals apart, or the dark night of the Eleusian cult, whose secrecy he swore over a lot of blood, I felt I was there. Usually each of them preformed a form of ritual violence, but rarely were they deemed to constitute any direct threat to the security of Rome. Indirectly was another matter, for in time, a group could provide a source of affirmation and a power base for those who would challenge Rome.

It was thus that I was surprised that Philo had not yet penetrated the Galilean sect and had but minimal clues as to their ways. Of course, he knew of the cursory entries regarding a certain Christos executed for high crimes of state, but as to specific mention of the 12, there was not an official trace. Other information—that they sacrificed infants and other unmentionable deeds, were not reliable, he said—only to show that they had powerful enemies.

"I knew as much," I said, knowing it would egg Philo on.

"There is one other thing. They use the remains of their dead in sacred rites."

"Yes, I have heard of their fascination with bones. It would match up with the reference to them being 'haters of the living.' But how can a secret burial clan be a threat to Rome?"

"Contact with the dead can lead to other aberrant practices," said Philo. "Blood is usually used to summon spirits."

"But in this case, bones. Just certain bones, especially those murdered––curious, not worth worrying about."

"Unless it be the bones of Imperial agents like yourself," mused Philo.

"That will not attract a large following. Rome is not barbaric."

Philo did not lead me to the first of the twelve, but a dream. It came as a vision, as a great winged bird, blood red, perhaps the Phoenix itself. Imprisoned in a pit of bones, its cage composed of bones, it broke through the bars and attacked me. I woke up in a cold sweat, checking my side for where the beast's beak pierced me. There was no wound.

Yet the dream provided a clue. When I told it to Philo, the next day—one of his specialties was dream augury––he said there was a place in Rome filled with bones and which also contained the living.

"You are sounding like an oracle," I said encouragingly.

"Have you forgotten the *Gemonium*? I hadn't thought until now, that it might be a place to look for spies."

As most of Rome knew, the Gemonium was a horrible rock pit, where the worst of her enemies were cast. No doubt, members of this sect had been thrown there, too. If something were to rise, might not it be one from there, perhaps an escaped prisoner?

We proceeded to the spot on the Capital where the Gemonium was encased under sold rock. It held two chambers, a temporary one for prisoners, and a second deeper chamber, a death cell. The jailers readily agreed to our passage into the first, which contained serious criminals and some who were insane. When I announced my intention to descend into the death cell, the jailers balked.

"No man comes out alive from there," they protested. Philo said that they were superstitious, believing evil spirits haunted there. "You'll catch the plague," one of the jailers warned.

At this point we showed our orders affixed with the seal of the emperor. They gave way and hurriedly showed me a rope attached to an iron ring. "One or two might still be alive," they said.

From a hole in the roof, we were lowered into the solid rock of the first chamber. The odor was oppressive and only narrow shafts of light penetrated, revealing several chained prisoners. Some began talking immediately, others were silent, and yet others uttered unintelligible syllables mixed with crazed laughter.

"A day in here would be enough to drive anyone mad," discerned Philo.

The prisoners cowered in the light of my torch, as if I was an apparition. "Are there followers of the Jew, Christos?" I called. There was an echoing answer, with a second voice adding an eerie punctuation to the first.

"The second chamber," Philo remarked, handing me an extra unlit torch.

With the rope around my waist, I proceeded through a jagged hole. Philo stayed above to insure my safe return. After lifting a circular stone, I exposed a narrow hole that led to utter dark. An indescribable fetid odor arose, and my torch burnt with a green tint as it mixed with the vapors.

A voice from below cried out, "Are you to descend the abyss and bring back the dead?"

Ignoring this demented comment, I lit the extra torch and threw it into the chamber below. The flame burst to twice its size, purifying the air. A pallid glow revealed disordered skeletons, and a shadowy form in the corner. "A cult of bones should feel at home, here," I called to Philo as I descended further. "Remember, the signal," shouted Philo. One jerk meant to proceed slowly down; two jerks meant stop. Repeated jerks meant to pull up immediately. My plan was to go down halfway and see what knowledge I could gain.

With torch in hand, I slowly descended. The walls were littered with unintelligible syllables, mostly Greek lettering, and I wondered how they had been placed this high. One inscription read *Ben Adam Echomenia,* a meaning I could not interpret. My eyes returned to below, and I was ten feet from the ground when I signaled Philo to stop. For some reason, I felt impelled to count the skulls. They were jumbled, and I lost count after a dozen, the strain on my eyes making the bones appear to move. The madness was descending on me, and I shook my head. To one side I saw the shadowy form take shape as a person. "No one has come out of here alive," I remembered the jailer saying. The man stared straight at me, his eyes having an uncanny intensity. I jerked the rope repeatedly, signaling Philo to bring me up.

The rope snapped, and I fell to the floor of bones. One slashed my upper leg. The light fell into a crevice and extinguished. Panic raced through me, as I expected to be attacked. I wheeled around, feeling for the rope above. It swung just out of reach. I yelled up to Philo for more rope, but the echoes were mixed with the crazed laughter of the madmen and made my words unintelligible. I realized he could see me, his eyes accustomed to the faintest light. Anything new in this chamber would stand out. I prepared to defend myself, but I had no weapon as they had been confiscated by the jailors.

I swung my hands around myself and above. I felt nothing. Suddenly, I was gripped from behind, then lifted up. The madman had great strength, and I could not resist. Philo's jest of the imperial investigator dying would become true after all, I feared, but my face brushed the rope. When I grasped it, the madman let go.

"Return from the dead," said what sounded like another voice. Then I realized it was the same person with different voices—and this one was the sane voice. I was released. I do not know why. Perhaps it was part of his fantasy. Jerking the rope several times, I was quickly spirited out of danger. On the way up, I cried out, "Who are you? Why are you here?"

"I am of two worlds," he answered enigmatically. "One with so much dark and one with so much light."

Philo, who had not made out any words, was relieved to see me unharmed. "A short visit to the underworld? What did you find out from below?"

I recounted the adventure, for which Philo seemed most interested in the Greek phrase, "It means, 'Come, Son of Man,'" he interpreted.

"What does that mean?"

"The Son of Man is a figure of light in their mythology. That may explain the madman's reference to the light."

"I don't know what we've gained if anything. There's a madman having visions of light. We might as well tell the emperor I'm the Phoenix rising from bones."

"Best not," warned Philo. "Jokes have shortened one's life before."

After emerging from the first prison, we queried the jailers who were playing a game of droughts. "Has any Christian been lifted from the Gemonium," I asked.

"None, except if you be Christian," one jested.

An older jailer corrected him. "Years ago, one came out with his insanity unchanged."

"I thought you said none had come out of the second," questioned Philo.

"There was an exception," reported the jailer. "The rulers have their fancies. This one was crucified in Nero's circus."

"His name," queried Philo.

"They called him Rock, no doubt because he survived so long in the pit. They say he was the leader of a cult."

"Where are his bones?" I asked.

"Ask the lions," said the jailers.

We left with news that the first of the twelve had died. "The problem is," I related to Philo, "is that this should be good news. But this oracle has gone to the emperor's head, and he'll worry more about one of the twelve becoming bones. It would have been better to find the man alive."

Philo suggested we check to see if there was a burial site and further clues at the Colosseum. "After all, the remaining eleven may have located his bones and use his burial site for their rituals. Still, it is puzzling. Maybe they don't ritually murder but incite the state to do it to them so they can use their bodies."

We went to the adjoining grounds of the circus in search of its burial site. A cacophony of sound came from animals and men, permeated with fear and unnatural excitement.

"Finding this man's remains is slim," I said. "There is unlikely to be any marked spot."

"And it's against the law to bury or recover the body of a condemned criminal."

"Does your imperial edict override such laws?" asked Philo.

"We could open the tomb of Caesar," I replied.

With provisions still being gathered for our ship to Delphi, we spent the remaining part of the week searching the tombs of Rome. We found nothing remarkable but heard reports that the sect did meet at night around certain tombs. On our last day, we searched Palatine Hill, the grounds littered with rocks and occasional bones. Mostly animal, though a human bone could be spied. We stopped to rest against an old boundary wall. For a moment I imagined the dead of this field rising––the animals, criminals, and the executed in a rage against Rome. Although such feelings struck me, I dismissed them as madness. "The dead cannot harm Rome," I muttered.

Squatting, Philo was staring at the wall. "More graffiti," he noted. He got up and searched the length of the wall, with mostly erotic drawings and words that befitted them. But in on the east side we found Greek symbols. Among them was one which caught his interest: the Greek letter Rho with a key-like form on the end.

"It looks like a code," said Philo.

"Or a good luck charm. People are always etching them onto walls and Rome's very monuments.

Philo dug his hand into the sandy marl and uncovered a white bone shard. "Unusual. It appears polished."

"Keep it for good luck."

"I don't believe in luck," said Philo.

At this point we heard chanting and tambourines from a road below us. "What is it?" I wondered.

"It's the Day of Blood," informed Philo. "The Cybele cult is having her spring feast. It's interesting to watch. Sometimes their activities get out of hand. It would be livelier to see than searching for more bones."

We departed, but I could help thinking we should have dug more around the sign of Rho. At the city's main causeway, priests of Attis were inflicting wounds on themselves. Their own God, who had castrated himself, was being processed into the temple. His body came as a cut-down pine, stuck with woolen fillets, and crowned with flowers. I couldn't help but look with repugnance at this Un-Roman group in the heart of our city. Yet it was her power, it was claimed, that helped us to counter the scourge of Carthage.

"Perhaps Rome has admitted a worst pestilence," I wondered.

Philo's mind was still elsewhere. "This Christian group holds their rights with real bones They are more difficult to interpret."

"And a wooden body is easier to find or make."

Philo laughed. "There is still a missing piece though." I laughed too, for he was referring to the shorn genitals of their god.

Our ship had set to sail, a fast-sailing warrior ship complete with twenty slaves to row if wind should fail us. As Rome receded in the distance, I had a strange foreboding. In the sky a cloud formation looked like a giant outstretched bird. I pointed it out to Philo, but he was not impressed.

"If it had been an eagle with a snake in its mouth, it would mean something." He handed me a list with twelve names on it. It had taken considerable work to obtain a fragment of the sect's writings. There were twelve suspects, of which one was confirmed dead. According to the oracle, only when all 12 died would the threat be posed. So, we must find one living.

CHAPTER III

MANNA BONES

The Tiber river led to the port of Ostia, where we received intelligence that a ship from Judea was coming through the straits to points unknown. Accompanied by an imperial galley, we set out to intercept it in the early morning.

The fog was thick when we reached the straits. Between the two ships, we cast a cord, for visibility was only a ship's length. The alien craft was not caught by our rope, however, but went to our starboard side. The galley looked whitened and was moving quickly. With our slave rowers at top speed, we overtook and hailed the ship. No one answered.

A boarding party prepared, and Philo and I joined them. Aboard, we opened the hatch and saw it was an escaped ship, filled with slaves. They bore marks on their bodies, scars from chains and whipping. Strangely silent, they offered no resistance.

"Where does this ship go?" I asked. There was no answer, but their eyes burned fiercely. Yet, I sensed no threat, as they were unarmed and showed no sign of violence. I ordered the ship searched, which turned up a meager supply of provisions. In one large wooden casket in the hold, we found a skeleton.

"An ill-fated member of the original crew?" asked the Triarch, who commanded the imperial galley. The bones, brilliant white, as if polished, had no head.

I asked whose remains they were, but none of the slaves answered.

I even offered their freedom, but not a word.

The Triarch Gaius was baffled that I would free slaves, and that I took such interest in bones. Still, he took charge, ordering, "Answer him, or I'll sink this ship!"

"The name is all I need, nothing more," I added, "and you may go free."

A broad-shouldered man from a back row called out, "We'll tell, if we can keep the remains."

"Keep your bones. Just give the name," I replied.

The man looked carefully at me, judging whether I would keep my word. Amazed, I wondered if these people would sacrifice themselves for a bag of bones.

"James the Less," he finally said.

Philo recalled the name as one of the twelve and asked, "What do you intend to do with the bones?" Again, we were met with silence.

"Perhaps we should cast them into the sea," said the Triarch Gaius. "If their rites gain strength from them."

"I gave my word."

"We should take a piece," said Philo to the side. "If they are collecting the twelve for purposes of sorcery, then our own magicians may use it to counter them."

I grabbed a clean white arm bone. What type of weapon was this in the hands of a slave crew? *Can this arm threaten Rome?* I closed the casket sharply. The absurdity of it disturbed me. With the soldiers I returned to our ship and ordered that the ship be allowed to pass wherever the wind took it. The galley ship returned to port, surely to tell a strange story.

The mist cleared as our ship entered the Adrian sea, and my spirits began to lift. Yet that very evening, there was another disturbing incident. In the hold where the soldiers had placed the bone, there came a scream. None of the soldiers would go below. When I inspected, I was surprised to find a stowaway, a slave woman. One of the soldiers must have secreted her aboard. My anger rose, for it was a promise broken. Although I had cause, I did not seek out the perpetrator. I took guard of the woman myself, lest she be abused and placed her in a nearby cabin.

She was young with beautiful, dark, braided hair. Not knowing her language, she was a silent companion. Although a slave, her face held dignity and communicated much with her eyes alone. I found myself treating her with care.

"Perhaps she can serve as an informant," said Philo later.

"I don't know the language she speaks, and she hardly speaks a word. It took me three days to find her name."

"She'll make a good slave-wife," jested Philo.

I corrected him. "She is a free woman now, and she will make her own choices."

Fair weather followed us toward the isles of Greece. Philo's eyes grew keener as we approached closer to those mystical cults which fascinated him. Finally, we landed and provisioned our horses for the journey inland to Delphi. Before setting out, we decided to inquire with the local governor regarding this sect.

The Governor of Patrae was irritated by my questions. "We've encountered them, too. In fact, I had one crucified, for he had set my wife against the household. It's a female cult," he went on with disgust. "They attract the weak."

The Governor was a follower of Mithra, a solar god with only male initiates. The cult's main image was the god putting a knife to the throat of a bull.

"If he is dead, we wish to inspect his bones," I said.

"Are you Christian too?" asked the Governor. "I don't keep track of bones."

"Maybe your wife knows?" asked Philo

The Governor rose from his chair. "She's in seclusion. No one may speak to her!"

Apparently, she had become infected with the Christian disease, but the Governor would not openly say.

When I showed my Imperial Orders, the Governor almost refused them. But as I guaranteed upmost confidentiality and assured that the emperor was only interested in the 12, he consented.

After being ushered past guards, we came upon the Governor's wife, looking forlorn and bright in aspect, with a measure of fight. She had been a native queen in the region. I was surprised that she and the slave girl were part of the same cabal. She was happy to speak about the cult but refused to reveal names of any followers.

"We are interested in the remains of one of the twelve," I informed. "We wish to inspect the bones and any marker by them."

By the look she gave us, she must have wondered if we were involved in the dark arts.

"It is to verify that he is dead," explained Philo. "We are imperial investigators."

"We have no wish to confiscate any bones," I added.

The woman, who longed to see the outside again and make a pilgrimage to her patron, agreed.

The Governor reluctantly consented but not without complaint. "It may agitate her further. Mentioning the emperor's interest will only lead her to believe that her superstition has truth."

By the seashore, the princes directed us to a rock-cut tomb in which bones had been laid under a heavy stone slab. When we raised the stone, no corruption emitted, only a faint fragrance of the original anointing.

"The limbs were not pierced, but he was crucified bound," Philo noted.

I picked up a bone and saw it looked fresh, as if marrow still coursed within.

"Manna flows from his bones," said the princess.

"Manna?"

"Food that our forefathers collected in the desert of Judah."

For a moment, the unexplained fragrance led me to consider how bones could be food.

"They are living bones," she went on.

Can these bones be living? I wondered. If so, they must be destroyed. But how can one kill bones? If you cut them up, there will be ten more. If you burn them, their ashes would be spread by the four winds. And it was from ashes the Phoenix was said to rise. The paradox had needled its way into me. Maybe the emperor was right, that something deeper lay here.

"Whose bones are these?" I asked.

"Andrew, brother of Peter."

"Another of the twelve," said Philo.

"Yes, the phoenix's birth is hastened," I added, unintelligibly to the woman. When she turned aside, I pocketed a finger bone, but the woman somehow sensed my action. She turned, looked at me wild eyed, and I feared she might leap upon me.

"We are bringing a sample to the emperor," I hastened to explain. "He too is interested in this cult."

The woman saw my half-truth, and I sensed her fury was barely contained. I didn't know where she placed it, and I didn't linger to find out.

Upset that I had lied, I told Philo later, "They bring it out of you. I'm a man of honor, yet I broke my word with them."

"Perhaps, you attach too much to your honor," Philo replied. "The governor has a point though. Although the twelve are men, underneath it's a female cult, compared to Mithra with its sun and seven golden steps marked by precious metals. This female cult revolves around bones claiming to be Manna, a type of food."

"What need is there for the emperor to worry, if the threat is only women?" I asked.

"If it were only ordinary women, but some, as you see, are from the house of governors. And women have been known to change the minds of men."

"Rome will never stoop to worshiping bones, or a mystery rite that feeds on them!"

"Perhaps, one day, it will be like the cult of Attis, imported when we felt a threat. A new threat will arise, and this new god will be invoked."

"It could happen," I allowed. "But Rome has swallowed much before and has stayed Rome."

"But I do not think Rome can swallow this one without being swallowed herself. There's something more than bones going on here."

"What is it then?"

"I don't know how to explain it. I sense it in their eyes, something that can't readily be put into words."

"Fierceness which does not carry a sword is no threat to Rome."

Philo paused, summoning from the depths of his arcane knowledge. "Therein lies the paradox. They are turning bones into swords."

CHAPTER IV

PROPHETESS OF DELPHI

The temple complex of Delphi was located atop an isolated, steep mountain, yet it held sway over kings and rulers. Although none could farm there, the blood of her sacrifices sprouted oracles from the Gods. "There was a time when it was human sacrifice," Philo informed.

"The Greeks are not barbaric."

"Cruder practices existed in earlier times, and they remember them in the remote hills. Have you seen the sculpted wolves beside the altars? Some say the first sacrifice was Apollo himself."

I held up my hands to the heavens. "Perhaps we should be honored to be the next sacrifice."

"You jest, but the imperial sword of Rome hangs over the Delphi elite. But we are not coming to collect gold, but an oracle."

After hours hiking up a long, winding trail, we reached the summit. To the attendant priests within the sacred precincts, we presented gifts and our petition––a carefully phrased request about how to stop this new cult. The priest conveyed our petition to the inner sanctum, and we awaited an oracle from the prophetess.

Philo had intelligence on the ritual mechanism. "The priestess sits over a primitive tripod. Myth has it that the Python's bones and teeth lay underneath. Some say it's the bones of Dionysus, and yet others Apollo."

"They are not so far from this Christian cult," I remarked. "Although we're looking for the bones of men, not a dragon snake or god."

"Bones may lead to bones," said Philo.

A goat was sacrificed, having first been dashed with cold water, causing it to quiver and signify assent. From within, we heard moaning, then bizarre, ecstatic sounds. Vapors came from the chamber at twilight, and the prophetess emerged. "Apollo has spoken:

Find the body of the Crucified One,
And the Phoenix will sleep a thousand more...."

"How are we supposed to find his body?" I asked, but the priestess did not respond, her eyes still glazed from trance.

"The Crucified One must refer to the cult's leader," said Philo. "His body disappeared, and according to their documents, descending into the underworld, then ascended into the sky."

"I'm not concerned about other worlds, but the length of the Roman world. How can we find this body?"

"He was crucified in Jerusalem. A good place to start...."

"But it could have been secreted anywhere. And what good is it if we find more bones?"

"If we find the bones of the crucified, it will disprove their myth that he rose from the dead. This is one case where they claim no bones. Perhaps they were hidden in a cave, or the body was burned, leaving only ashes."

"What harm can come from bones and ashes," I objected again. "The soul separates from the body at death. The vital force has left."

"In our belief. Perhaps they have found a way to make the soul cling to the body. There are certain incantations ... It would explain the fragrance and the glowing white quality."

"Let us not even partly buy into this cult!" I objected. "The original oracle told us that bones of the twelve were the threat, not the founder's missing body."

"But this new oracle offers a way to stop the twelve. The missing body would probably be in Jerusalem."

"We will go to Alexandria of Egypt first," I decided. "I have intelligence that a certain Matthew passed through there. I would like to talk to one of the 12 who are living, before time runs out. The bones of the Crucified One aren't going anywhere."

We left Delphi with a votive statue, and to complete our bone ensemble, Philo took a burnt piece from the sacrificial goat.

We arrived at port to find our ship replenished and all in order, except for a report that the former slave woman, Kentra, had been acting strangely.

"She was trying to enter your quarters, saying it's the only safe place," said Gaius.

I found her in the hold, wild eyed, half-clothed and bound to a post. Around lay clothes she had shredded. She appeared to be a mad woman.

I loosened the bonds. She was silent, then flung herself at me. I put my cloak over her, wondering how could manage a mad woman at close quarters for a long voyage. After a while, she quieted, and I brought her back to her room.

On deck I demanded to know what had happened, but an officer in charge said nothing had. "Slaves go crazy," he said. "The whip cures them, sure enough."

I consulted Philo, who said, "Having escaped from slavery, to be caught again, and the fear of being sent back has disturbed her mind."

"I will return her to her homeland and insure she has her freedom."

"In this state she's in, and without any protector? You must wean her into freedom. Maybe a Roman matron will protect her upon our return."

"But we can't have a mad woman at our heels for weeks. She just tore up her clothes."

"Slave clothes," said Philo.

I wondered if her action had made sense. "Still, it could get worse. Who knows what she will tear up next...?"

Philo was on the side of keeping her. "Her mania may come in useful. After all, it is a mad enterprise we are set upon."

I ordered someone ashore to buy women's clothes of good quality. The emperor had given us a healthy account, and soon I had a princes on my hands. The clothes affected her demeanor, her fierce pride returned. She even became haughty, ordering the men to provide things for her. I told the men to humor her as much as possible. From then on, her language skills increased, as she realized she could get her needs met. The men understood that an Imperial agent can have his own woman but were mystified by my choice. Rumor said she had noble blood in her, and they referred to her as Princess. She stayed in her own quarters but did not hesitate to visit mine.

One early morning she awoke me by digging about my things. My bone collection lay scattered on the floor. She had grasped something in her hand and was hitting it against a metal fitting. "It's hexed!" she cried. Pieces of Delphic goat bone were sent flying.

I grabbed the bone from her hand, but not before its edge cut my palm. Angry, I struck her arm. The look she returned was so fierce that for a moment I feared for my life. But she saw the shame in my eyes for hitting a woman --the first time I had--and did nothing.

Above and at the rear of the ship, I found Philo looking out to sea. "It's out of hand," I said, after telling about the incident. "This woman is too much."

"She is superstitious. She fears objects that spirits may inhabit."

"I fear she may become violent."

"You could leave her bound in the hold," suggested Philo.

"I don't trust the hands on board."

"The emperor would not be pleased if his Imperial agent fell by the hand of an assassin of this cult. You know the way he thinks. It would redouble his fears and end up hurting hurt Rome."

"I will not die by hers," I said. Then, for some reason, the image appeared in my mind of the Phoenix piercing my breast.

CHAPTER V

KENTRA

It was a long voyage, and Kentra tried my patience more than once. I was tempted to leave her at a port or sell her back to a slave ship. But I was her only guardian now and felt duty bound to shield her. So, I kept secret disturbing details of her behavior. Only with Philo did I somewhat confide, and he appeared thoroughly puzzled as to the meaning of her actions. When I entered her cabin to check on her, a burnt odor sometimes filled her room.

"Perhaps she engages in a secret ritual," suggested Philo.

Her behavior on deck was obviously troubled. She would stare at the sea for hours, and weep uncontrollably. Occasionally her frenzied speaking ran on about the evils of the empire, the conspiracy of Rome against the world, and how Rome was in league with demons. Everyone realized she was not of right mind and wondered why an Imperial agent was protecting her. Nonetheless, the crew tolerated a well-dressed, attractive woman on board a ship for a long voyage.

One day, she started a small fire in her cabin. It was simply good fortune that I was nearby and put it out.

"What are you doing?" I screamed.

She was silent, bent over with her long hair and hands over her face. I pressed her till she finally said, "I'm getting rid of the hex in my hair."

I noticed singed hair among curled pieces of map she had burnt. "Why? What's wrong with your hair?"

"They were in a gray strand I found."

"They?"

At this moment the Triarch and his next in command entered, having smelled the fire from above. "Send her down to the hold," ordered Gaius. "There is no choice."

Kentra had been locked below for several hours, when toward evening, I checked on her. She was pale in the face––only a trace of the fiery glint in her eyes. *Could a few hours in the hold do this?* I wondered. Then I noticed lines of blood from wounds on her arms.

I hurried above and called the second in command.

"The ship's doctor took some of her fire from her, by letting blood," he revealed.

"He almost killed her!" I shouted.

"It's worked, hasn't it? She has hardly screamed and has not the strength to do anything else."

I hurried to the Triarch and demanded to know why he had not asked me first about the treatment.

"My first duty is to my ship," he simply said.

"It doesn't mean you have to kill her! The doctor is due to come back and let more blood!"

"We could leave her untreated and keep her chained below indefinitely. But I thought medical treatment is preferable, to see if it works. The doctor relieves the pressure, so that the humor doesn't get out of control."

"She's being depleted of blood and expected to hold her own against the rats and galley slaves?"

My statement had no effect, so I pulled out my only real card. "She is connected to a cult that the emperor has asked me to investigate. The future of Rome may be at stake."

"Yes, I know you have sweeping orders. But it's hard to believe how a former slave woman can help Rome. Indeed, she rails against Rome during her fits. Still, I can leave all that to your judgement. But when you make her queen of this ship, and she starts fires to be rid of demons, it's gone too far."

It was a touchy situation, the lines of authority not so clearly drawn. Although I was Friend of the Emperor, my position was not defensible if the ship was endangered. "Let me bring her up and watch her for three days and see if my way keeps her calm," I negotiated. "If she hasn't calmed down...."

"One day," inserted the Triarch. "In three days we could be at the bottom of the sea. Have someone constantly watch her."

I was faced with healing the woman, but I didn't know about such matters. Her condition had only worsened since her time in the hold. Before, she had some measure of stability in an alien world with the assurance that I could protect her. Now she sensed the limits of my power and thought the demons were breaking through.

Philo, however, said he knew certain indigenous healing rituals. "Either they think of madness as a small red demon within them, or a black demon who has stolen their mind. We could try to kill the red demon or steal back her mind from the black one."

"We're not magicians."

"I know of ceremonies...."

Philo tried an elaborate incantation, but it wasn't convincing enough and his effort failed. Kentra became more scared, and she accused Philo of trying to hex her.

"I'll hex the Roman World. I'll burn it up!" she cursed. "And this ship, too. It will all burn up!" Then she lapsed into a brooding silence.

At one point I asked what she was thinking about or planning to do.

"Revenge," she answered.

Her condition was worsening but locking her in the hold would only spiral her further into madness from which she might not return.

"What about the bones?" asked Philo. "If she believes they are magical, they may have an effect."

"She destroyed the Delphi bone."

"Try the finger bone from Patrae," said Philo.

The bone and a ritual Philo improvised worked. At first when we presented the bone, Kentra shook like she was having a convulsion, then she markedly calmed. After donning it around her neck, she took off her noble clothes and wore a simple robe. "Why didn't we think of this before?" I asked.

"The Bone Cult," named Philo.

CHAPTER VI

THE ALEXANDRIAN CULT

We were still miles out to sea when we spied the top of the famous lighthouse of Alexandria. First seen upside down as in a mirage, its 500-foot spire was shrouded in the morning mist. The port was busy even at this early hour, as ships laden with wheat were constantly leaving for Rome.

Our Imperial orders gained us an audience in the palace with the Governor of Egypt that same morning.

"I have not heard of a Bone Cult," said the Governor. "As for the Phoenix, it is nothing more than a legend."

"Egypt is the source of the legend. Surely you can inform us more about it," I persisted.

The Governor summoned an Egyptian priest to tell the story. Dressed in white linen, it appeared to follow old ways.

"It is a great, red-gold bird," the priest described. "After the Phoenix lays down and dies, she is consumed by her own fire. Then she rises from the dead, takes her own ashes, and bones, and lays them upon the altar at Heliopolis."

I let the impossibility of the story go and asked, "Are there bones there now?"

"The altar is clean. The Phoenix comes but once every 1000 years. Some say the time is near for its arrival."

When I asked the Governor if a watch could be placed at the altar, he was puzzled.

"We think this cult is making use of the Phoenix myth, applying it to their founder," explained Philo.

"We are concerned that one of his 12 main followers may make an appearance, claiming to be him," I added. "We suspect one of the twelve, a certain Matthew, is here."

Philo and I were surprised the Governor knew of him. "Yes, this man healed the daughter of a local noble and was permitted to travel into Upper Egypt. From there, he went to Ethiopia. It is unusual for Jews to do such."

"He is one from the Bone Cult that started in Jerusalem."

"It is a strange cult that starts in the hills of Judea and goes to the source of the Nile."

"They have divided the world among themselves," Philo informed.

"They sent two men to conquer Ethiopia?" asked the Governor.

I did my best to explain. "The Bone Cult conquers by gaining a following among the native peoples, claiming to perform miracles and doing favors for people in power."

"Who is the second person?" asked Philo, but the Governor didn't know.

It was hard to tell if the Governor was taking us seriously. "If they are so dangerous, perhaps they are better left in Ethiopia," he said.

"Can you tell us about Ethiopia?" I asked.

"They're barbarians claiming to have kings. The land has its share of volcanoes and lions."

Our audience ended, and the Governor refused to put a guard on Heliopolis, saying it was unwarranted. "Unless you can find evidence that this Jewish cult is engaged in treasonous activity," he qualified.

We let it go, and Philo decided to make use of our time in Alexandria by visiting its famous library.

I went to check on Kentra. Things had deteriorated again. She even became angry and suspicious of me

"She must go," said Gaius. "When we let her loose, she wanders aimlessly. If she doesn't first destroy the ship, she will fall overboard. Some men have tried to take advantage of her."

Nothing, it seemed, would change the Triarch's mind. Perhaps he sensed my authority diminished the further we got from Rome.

"What do you want me to do?" I asked.

"There's a slave ship heading to Jerusalem tomorrow. Put her aboard."

"Jerusalem is in ruins. How can we send someone in her condition there?"

Gaius suggested a house prison in Joppa, the port to Jerusalem.

When I approached Kentra with the idea of going home, she overcame her fear of me and clung to me.

But my power had its limits. In the end I was forced to agree. I did so, only after having talked with the slave ship's Triarch, who insured her safe care in Joppa, with a handsome reward promised.

"Some of her fears will be confirmed when I do this," I told Philo later. "But I see no choice."

We were at the library, and Philo was distracted.

"Have you found anything? Any clue to the mystery?" I asked.

"There may be a Jewish Phoenix after all," Philo replied. "A visionary writer named Enoch describes a being of light who accompanies the sun––a composite beast with the feet of a lion and head of a crocodile. It's of immense size, red color and has 12 wings."

"Twelve again? Perhaps a dream apparition from a member of a cult ... What could a crocodile head mean?"

"This was written decades before the cult appeared. As for the crocodile ... In apocalyptic writing, it's the symbol for a Great Beast that will rise and attempt to swallow Rome."

"It all sounds like a bizarre code. I think we need to reassess what's happening. Usually, my job is to go in search of a traitor or an assassin. Here, the traitor has already been killed by the state. No mystery thus far, except the body goes missing. His key followers, so far, have either died violent deaths or gone missing. And their bones are important."

"As the oracle predicts."

"Further, it also appears that this cult makes significant friends and enemies wherever it goes. It has a strange attraction and repulsion among important people. It's a dangerous madness."

"Let me add to this," said Philo. "Their leader's body has disappeared and is said to be risen from the dead. The 12 key followers are becoming victims, yet the oracle says they will be the source of the Phoenix that will one day rule Rome. How can we stop victims? One victim becomes 12, becomes 144, and so on. If victims feed the cult––they worship their bones––the more we kill, the more it will grow."

"Ingenious," I said. "If victims produce more followers, soon they will engulf the state. And Rome will be become powerless to stop them. Rome will become them, and all without one act of violence. What are we to do?"

"Take one alive, don't rashly kill him. Gain knowledge of the cult and then discredit it. Above all, we must find one alive."

"Even if we have to go beyond Rome, to Ethiopia," I affirmed. "At least we have time. At this rate, it would take hundreds of years to conquer Rome."

"But what if the original case was a mistake," Philo suddenly asked. "What if Rome was wrong?"

"The state doesn't crucify lightly," I answered. "But the matter is settled and done, even if Rome was wrong. The question is, where do we go from here?"

"First, we find his following in Alexandria," suggested Philo, "and make enquiries before going to the ends of the earth. We can look for a Christian prophet to find out how the second phoenix will rise."

CHAPTER VII

THE AGED SCRIBE

"The task will be harder than you imagine," Philo warned. "They have no obvious temples, but have infiltrated synagogues, the Jewish wisdom schools. Two of the cities' five quarters are Jewish with dozens of temples. Lately, they've been persecuted from the uprising and will be wary of any investigator.

"Let's try the tombs first. They have not failed us in providing clues."

"Tombs. I'm taking a liking to them," said Philo.

We passed marshes near the Nile and saw flocks of red flamingos rise in waves. Great blue herons stood on small, isolated mounds. "Notice, how the heron's legs are red," said Philo. "It's their mating season."

"Perhaps, it's the original bird of their Phoenix legends," I wondered.

Beyond the city outskirts, we found burial grounds with stones bearing typical Jewish markings. Some of the bird engravings were ibex-like, which Philo suspected of being Christian. "Let's dig up one of these," he proposed.

I was disturbed by the prospect of digging up graves. "It's but a faint clue."

"They're oriented to the sun," observed Philo. "The Bone Cult is oriented to the rising sun."

We hired a beggar to exhume the grave, and the unpleasant task was soon over.

"There's nothing here but bones with a gypsum coating," I said. The pale gray-white powder had a red undertone.

"Therein lies the clue," said Philo. "No coin in the mouth for Charon, no grave goods, no extra pair of boots. They don't plan for the dead to have a regular body with all its needs. Rather it will be changed...."

"Lack of goods is the sign of a poor man."

"Or the sign of the Phoenix-Bone Cult. Our custom is to keep the dead out of the city and out of view. But this cult seeks to give dead wings, with images of birds, direction to the dawning sun, and with coatings of white."

"They would haunt the earth," I hastily dismissed.

"I think they envision another land where their new bodies go."

"Let them have their new land. It is only the living who pose a threat to Rome."

"There are ways to ask the dead," revealed Philo.

"We are not desperate," I said, realizing him to be serious.

When we returned to the city, Philo commented, "We're defiled according to their custom."

"Yes, we could use a good washing at the baths," I suggested.

"It is the Jews who wash before everything, but a relaxing bath is in order."

The afternoon was spent in the great baths, where we gained a piece of intelligence. "It is no great secret," gossiped the man, his obesity being a sign of wealth. He was hoping to curry favor, when he found we were agents of the emperor. "I know a group of them. They meet in a friend's house, named Silas. He's inclined to follow crazy fashions. I've tried to warn him that he's taking this too far, so he doesn't invite me to their parties." The man seemed more bothered by this rejection than possible disloyalty to Rome.

That very evening, we knocked on the door and gained admittance as two seekers. Silas was hospitable, but told little of the cult, saying he was a novice and had not yet seen their inner mysteries.

"We are looking for one willing to share their wisdom," I persisted. "Can you help us?"

"Let us have dinner," he answered, as if still considering the matter. We had supper where poor and rich ate together. It was unusual, but I spoke easily with both groups, as my investigations taught me that sources can come from unlikely places.

After dinner, Silas gave his agreement. "You may talk to the scribe." He showed further into to the house, an inner room where an aged man sat on an elaborately carved chair. He was transcribing text onto a papyrus parchment.

"We are seekers," began Philo. "We have heard that the new Phoenix is about to rise."

"One has risen already," the scribe answered.

"From where?"

"Jerusalem."

"Do you know this by oracle?" asked Philo.

"Some have seen and touched him," the man answered.

"Have you heard of the twelve?" I asked, but realizing that this question sounded interrogatory, Philo added, "We wonder if the Phoenix is divided into twelve, to be gathered together."

"The Phoenix is a venerable Egyptian myth. But this is not a myth." The scribe pulled out a parchment and read:

In the regeneration, when the Son of Man sits on his throne of glory,
There will be twelve thrones judging the twelve tribes....

It was startling to hear evidence from their sources, which seemed to confirm the phoenix oracle from Delphi. "When will this come to pass?" I asked.

"This very generation," said the scribe.

"When the apostles are bones," I said as an aside. "Do you know that private collections of oracles are illegal?"

A tense moment passed. The man must have realized we were Roman agents.

"I too am prepared to die," was his reply.

We politely made our exit, and I was left disturbed. "Yesterday, we were grave diggers, and today we are perceived as assassins to an aged man. This assignment is becoming more and more bizarre," I confided to Philo.

'At least we have found one living, though he's aged. There is some time still...."

I laughed, wondering if Philo actually took this group as a serious threat.

Philo was unperturbed. "We have confirmation of treasonous activity. It has come together. Their own scriptures say there is to be a second regeneration, a new Phoenix rising, and it's based on the twelve."

"But I gather this Son of Man is of another world, not this one ... What does Rome have to fear?"

"They have a prayer which says, 'On earth as it is in heaven.'"

"So they wish," I retorted.

Over the next few days, we wandered the streets of Alexandria. On Sunday we knew the cult would gather at the scribe's house and decided to attend. We needed more evidence. The Governor would hardly take some obscure oracle from years ago as a threat.

At the city's center, we stopped at a huge monument. It was Alexander's tomb, the founder and *Soter* of the city. "Could this cult really rival the Savior here?" I asked. "Alexander conquered the world. What has their leader done? He has gained twelve to convert the world and sent them on death missions...."

Philo responded enigmatically. "The future is hard to see. Signs of it are invisible at first, then the faintest signs...."

A frenzied procession interrupted our conversation. A native cult filled the street, crying out laments. Prayers were punctuated with lacerations of arms, opening old scars. "What crazed cult is this?" I asked.

"The followers of Osiris. They're lamenting a missing body and go in procession, pretending to hunt for it."

"A missing body again?" I asked.

"In their legend, Osiris was cut into 13 pieces. Twelve were found, except for the virile member which was thrown into the Nile."

"There it was eaten by the Great Crocodile," I jested.

Philo considered for a moment. "I do not think they say what happened. Perhaps we too are going after the 12 and missing the central one."

"What do you mean?" I asked, beyond his errant pun.

"I have said it before. We should seek out this Son of Man, who is supposed to have left no bones. But if we find them, we can discredit the cult before it is too late."

"How can we find one person's bones in all of Rome? And if we did, how can we prove they are his?"

"Perhaps it is hopeless, among the living," Philo replied.

"There is something more the scribe did not tell us," I pursued. "If we but knew the right questions to ask, he would speak the truth."

"Perhaps he knows where the body of the Crucified One was last laid."

The next morning we went to Silas's house with our request, only to find the aged man had died that night. "There's no clue as to the cause of the death," said Silas. "He was writing."

"What were his last words?" asked Philo.

"It wasn't his usual transcription," revealed Silas. "He was writing poetry, which he sometimes does. I don't know what it means, but I will read it:

Under the temple's shattered stones,
A fish swims with whitened skin...."

"A white fish under the temple?" I questioned. "We were looking for a Phoenix."

"It's another guise of their leader," informed Philo. "Perhaps his underworld aspect." "Tell me, Silas, under which temple stones should we search?"

"It has to be the Great Temple in Jerusalem."

Philo confirmed. "Jerusalem is the origin of the cult, and she has a shattered temple. It's time we went there."

"And give up on Matthew?"

"The scribe you talked to was he," revealed Silas.

The next day, I shared a dream and some thoughts with Philo. "This whole affair has become a riddle. Lately, one has entered my head. It came to me after I remembered a dream. I was spearing fish and then heard the message. It doesn't make much sense."

"What was the message?"

"Spear the fish, and the Phoenix will rise."

"Their fish, if it stands for their leader, has already been speared," mused Philo. "And they claim he has already risen."

"There's something more. When I speared the fish, a pain came to my chest. It doesn't make sense."

Philo looked at me quizzically. "You are both slayer and slain? Perhaps you will rise too, like the Phoenix? Don't tell me you're to become the 13th follower and victim as well!"

CHAPTER VIII

JERUSALEM

We landed in Joppa, the nearest port to Jerusalem, bypassing the great imperial city of Caesura. While our ship was being overhauled, we would make an overland trip to Jerusalem. Before we left, I tracked down Kentra. I found she had become a high-class slave to a wealthy merchant.

Although the stern discipline of the merchant made her appear better, the shock of returning to slavery had worsened her in other ways. Her eyes would take on a vacant look as she whispered about the return of shadow ghosts and demons, and even believe we were their agents. I decided on the spur to buy her back, else she permanently descends into madness. She had become conversant in our language and could serve as a translator. The merchant relented after hearing my sum and knowing of my connection to the emperor. The Triarch Gaius, upon hearing of my return and perhaps feeling guilty himself, granted us a soldier named Praeces, who would ease our burden of caring for her. I knew, however, the decision was irrational and might slow us down....

The trip was due west, climbing up from a coastal plain, and becoming arduous as we entered the mountains. Fortunately, a Roman road lay beneath our feet, and a bright blue sky above. Days later, we reached the pass of Hurun and saw the City perched on the heights. "An apt nest for the Phoenix," Philo commented.

Jerusalem looked good only from a distance. As we neared, the smell of smoke seemed to still hang in the air. Wayside tombs were upturned, and breached walls littered the ground with broken stones. The Temple itself was completely razed, leaving but the stone mount upon which it had stood.

Upon the sight, Kentra broke down into uncontrolled sobbing, so we left her in the lower city with Praeces. We did not leave the wailing behind, however, for along a section of wall still standing dozens of Jews were crying due to the demise of their holy site.

The 10th Roman Legion was still garrisoned on the mount, lest a revolt stir again. When we asked the centurion about the burial of the Crucified One, any clues to the whereabouts of where his following might be buried. He shrugged. "Hundreds have been crucified, and we don't permit burial."

"What of the temple––has all worship stopped?" asked Philo.

"You'll find a few rootless beggars and mourners from the countryside. It's impossible to stop them. But wails are easier to endure than these constant petitions." He was obviously not happy with his assignment, seeing himself more suited for the battlefield than guarding ruins.

"You may go to the Temple Mount and see for yourself. Be wary of strange types attracted there, from beggars to lunatic prophets. Sometimes, I think it would have been better to let the Temple stand than to have what it's breeding."

"Have you heard of the Phoenix myth?" it occurred for me to ask.

"The only birds of late are those," he said, pointing to huge griffin vultures circling above.

We worked our way up through the haze and immediately came upon what the centurion predicted. A ghostly apparition, a man with a crazed look, was wheeling about in loose robes. "I am He," he was shouting. By his side stood a beautiful woman, dressed in the clothes of a courtesan. A few pilgrims had stopped to listen to this nonsense.

"Could this be the new phoenix rising from Jerusalem's ruins?" Philo asked.

"If we bring him to the emperor, his counselors will have a good laugh."

"I am he who is to come!" he cried out.

I approached him. "Your name?"

A hint of sanity returned to his eyes. "Faustus, the favored one!"

"We are looking for one crucified and his 12 followers."

"You look for corpses when life is here," he said, extending his arm to the woman.

"Who is she?" I asked.

"The first idea of my divine mind."

"Not a bad idea," I mocked-complimented. "What others do you have?"

"Better ones than to hunt for bones."

The man had clearly identified and pointed out our absurdity, so he wasn't all mad.

"If you are a god," said Philo. "Tell us, *where* will the Phoenix rise?"

"No! It will not rise again!" he screeched. "The worm will not make a new bird, for a great beast will come and swallow the worm. There will be no rising!"

"And who is this beast?" I pursued.

"You will wish to know things that it is best not to know. For it will come in the dead of the night and kill you," he prophesied. With that, Faustus left, with his woman in tow.

His threat left me unsettled. Although I knew it was no more than his other maniacal ravings, I could not readily make it leave my mind.

"Magicians like him can only conjure an apparition or two," consoled Philo.

"Yet, the man is disturbing. I believe he dabbles in some deeper magic."

"The destruction of a sacred site with all the spilled blood stirs dark forces," allowed Philo. "There's——"

"Enough of this discussion!" I interrupted. "We dwell too long on this."

In the morning, we met with the centurion again. "There is no gold there," he said, incredulous when I announced our intention of digging under the temple. "The cherubim have long been taken."

"We are looking for graves there," corrected Philo. "Do you know of any?"

The centurion shook his head and called for his Jewish informant.

"Underneath there are empty vaults," he revealed. "They were dug out of fear that there may be hidden graves below."

"Could a secret cult be using one of the ancient vaults?" I asked.

"The precincts are guarded," informed the centurion, impatient with my line of questioning. "Perhaps a few hermits have made their way in there, however."

I insisted we be allowed to search, reminding him of our imperial edict. Despite the ire this might raise from the local populace, the centurion agreed.

"I will give you workmen soldiers to hasten your task," the centurion offered. "Dig as much as you want. But I can assure you, all the treasures are gone."

The following day we began the unlikely project. The temple area was immense, and the question arose as to where to dig. Philo said one must go by their gut in this matter. He walked about, sensing the ground, and stopped at a point near where Faustus had stood.

The day's work was uneventful, except for two things. In the morning, we spotted a Jewish spy viewing our project, but he ran off before he could be captured. And in the afternoon, a broken limestone block was uncovered with an inscription in Latin and Greek:

*Whoever is caught will have himself
to blame for his death, which will follow....*

The builders had sought to protect the holy site by a curse.

"The Temple is already desecrated and broken," I said.

Philo was more concerned about the spy who had escaped than any ancient curse. "If he informs a radical Jewish sect that we've been tampering with their sacred site, we could become a target."

At the end of the day, aside from the inscribed block, we found a broken menorah, a few animal bones, and burnt pieces of temple furnishings.

Back in our quarters, I studied a map which only outlined the boundaries of the temple. My frustration was building. "The Temple Mount is too immense. There must be a way of gaining intelligence to locate the vaults. Otherwise, this could take weeks."

Philo was intently studying another document.

"What does it read?" I asked.

"I have found a reference to the temple in a letter written to the cult's following.

*He entered the Holy of Holies,
where his body made a fresh and living way...."*

"It raises the interesting possibility," Philo speculated. "The Bone Cult may have placed the founder's body in the inner sanctum, hoping to rebuild the temple one day around it."

"Then we need to locate the inner sanctum."

"The centurion said the Jews would rather die than reveal the sacred spot."

"Maybe Kentra can help us," I suggested.

"Women were only allowed in the outer courtyard," Philo informed. "But she might know the general area."

Early the next day, we took Kentra to the Mount, and she trembled atop the ruins. It was a risk that bringing her here might activate her insanity. But as she came to an area which was especially scarred, she knelt down. We signaled the workmen.

It was not long in digging before they broke through to a cave chamber. We had come to Jerusalem's most holy spot, for we could see pieces of the winged Cherubim laying about. *Would this be the spot from which the Phoenix would arise?* Philo and I descended through the opening and examined the chamber which had a narrow cut shaft, leading yet deeper.

"It's a burial shaft," Philo discerned, "long before the temple was here."

With Philo holding a lit torch above and using a rope, I descended the shaft, and saw it opened into a shallow chamber, small and cramped. Not a single bone or inscribed message was there, only a piece of cloth which I folded and placed under my belt. "If the Phoenix was here, it fled," I said upon coming up.

Once outside the vaults and in the daylight, we inspected the cloth. Purple, it was fringed with gold and torn on one side.

Silent until now, Kentra grabbed the cloth and said, "His death caused the temple veil to tear."

I did not ask how a death could do this, rather, "Can you tell us where the body was placed?"

She pointed across the valley. "The Mount of Olives. He ascended from there."

"Another mound to dig," I sighed.

"What's on the Mount of Olives?" I asked the centurion later.

"Gardens and oil presses. Sometimes radical groups meet there in secret. They plot the death of any unguarded Roman they can find."

CHAPTER IX

A BEGGAR

The Mount of Olives was a dome-shaped hill east of the Temple Mount. "A cemetery is there too," said the centurion. "But I doubt if you'll find much of importance. The dead do not bother Rome."

"It's an aberrant cult," Philo explained, "who have turned fear of bones into their worship."

"Bones aren't swords or spears. Why is the emperor so concerned? Perhaps, he has an attraction to the cult."

"The emperor's concern is about fanaticism," I corrected. "Nothing may have come of them as yet, but the cult prophesies the overthrow of Rome." The centurion laughed, saying that prophecy comes easily and doesn't feed soldiers. Busy with correspondence, he sent an underling to accompany us for our safety.

"From the top, fire signals are still used to mark the beginning of their feasts," the soldier informant told us.

Along the western slopes, the once luxuriant olive groves had been cut down and bore only a few new growths. The cemetery, however, had been left undisturbed. Tombs were plentiful, but none of the white-washed shrines bore any inscriptions suggestive of the cult. The informant suggested we ask a hermit that lived on the Mount. "I've heard him raving," he said. "Saying the temple's destruction was their God's judgement."

We proceeded south to a small round shaped hill, exposed to a sharp wind. "The Belly of the Winds," related the soldier-informant. A few of the rock-cut tombs appeared inhabited, for stone circles held the ashes of extinguished fires.

The informant yelled into one such tomb, and soon a beggar wearing a goat skin emerged.

"Do you know of the Christian cult?" I asked, but the man didn't answer. Even after translation, he did not appear to comprehend.

"Perhaps he doesn't know the word. Do you worship the one whose body is claimed to be missing?" asked Philo.

Still, the beggar showed no sign of recognition. Only when we described the type of death that the man had undergone, and the claims afterward did he make the cult's sign of over his face.

"He's one of the death worshipers," said the informant.

"Ask him if he has any friends," I requested, but the beggar remained mum to the question. We waited, wondering what to do next.

"If this is the type of followers this man who is claimed to be god has, why do you worry?" asked the informant.

"Therein lies the riddle," said Philo. "From royal houses to beggars in caves––the very range of attraction."

"Tombs, do you know of any Christian tombs?" I persisted.

The beggar pointed to a field. An ancient, bowed oak stood in the middle, its side scarred by lightning.

"The Blood Field," said the translator. "I don't know why it is so named, for no battle was fought here. The land is haunted."

"I remember. There is an association to one of the twelve," Philo said. "One died there."

"Are you going to try to dig up this field too?" asked the informant. "Its rocky surface is unbroken, and any body laid there––its bones have long since scattered."

The beggar suddenly spoke, revealing that he knew much. "The betrayer was of the Sicarii, who have the sign of Cain."

I threw the beggar a golden coin for his words, but he let it lie on the ground, as if tainted. I couldn't understand his refusal, for he obviously lived in extreme poverty. On impulse, I gave him my cloak. He stared at me, then took off his goatskin and handed it to me. I couldn't refuse.

On our way back to the city, Philo wondered what I was going to do with the goat skin.

"Perhaps it will come in useful for a disguise," I mused. "Our professional apparel does not carry us far with this cult."

Back at the camp, we found that there had been trouble regarding Kentra. "She struck a Roman Officer," the centurion reported.

"Was there a reason?" I asked. "Was he making advances?"

The centurion angered. "Why do you worry about a woman who was once a slave to Rome? She tempts my men, talking to them freely and not offering anything other than tales about a new religion."

He, too, was a friend of Caesar, and there was nothing I could do if he chose to detain her. An appeal to the emperor on her behalf could take weeks.

Still, the centurion was no fool. He knew I was on personal terms with the emperor himself and let it go at a warning. "Talk to this woman and see that it does not happen again."

I had a talk with Kentra. "You have to be careful. Women here don't mix with soldiers, unless they're of low character."

This set off one of her tirades. "I am not your slave! And I am not dead! Why can't I do things like a man?"

"Behave or I'll take away your bone charm!" I threatened.

It only made her angrier. She tore off the charm, threw it down, and rushed outside. I watched her descend into the city and didn't try to stop her.

That night I slept uneasily, wondering what would happen to Kentra.

In the morning, however, a knife mark on my door gave me another worry. The mark made a design I couldn't interpret. *Had Kentra come back and placed a hex on me?* I wondered.

In my morning talk with the centurion, I informed him of Kentra's disappearance and showed him a copy of the sign.

"It's the Sicarii," he said.

"I have heard their name. Tell me more."

"They're assassins, named from their curved Parthian knives. Isolated gangs still roam the countryside and assassinate soldiers. Perhaps the Sicarii think you have come to investigate them and have sent a warning."

"Was not Masada their last outpost?"

"Yes. Our legions reduced it to flames. Rather than surrender, they killed themselves, over a thousand."

"Did any survive?"

"A few women and children escaped. They sprout up like hydra. If there is a cult to worry about, it's that one."

Later that day I conferred with Philo. He didn't recognize the sign, but he said it looked coded and suggested I sleep in new quarters.

"Maybe the centurion is right. The Sicarii, the cult of the knife, is the real threat, not the cult of whited and perfumed bones," I speculated.

Philo, however, remained alert to the more exotic danger. "Rome has always dealt well, if ruthlessly, with armed threats. But bones? Rome fears them enough to place her burials outside her city. If they brought bones into the City of Rome, maybe it is a way to overthrow Rome. I have heard rumors of their catacombs under the city."

"We need more facts," I said, shaking my head. "We do know the way of the knife. But these bones of the dead are being used in rituals which draw different social classes together... That may pose a danger to the very fabric of Rome. The beggar's words were few, but his actions were great. I am going to put his skin to infiltrate the cult."

CHAPTER X

THE SICARII

The next morning I worked the transformation, donning the goatskin, cutting my hair raggedly. I dirtied my face with ashes and wore Kentra's bone charm around my neck.

"You look the part. Nobody will bother you much now," Philo complimented. "But must you wear the bone? I wonder if it doesn't drive one crazy."

"Then I will become a little crazed and less suspected."

Wandering through the old city as a beggar, I found myself looking for signs of the Christian cult and for Kentra. Her disappearance disturbed me more than I expected, and I frequented areas where a lost woman might be—the soldier's brothel, the slave market, and begging places. Each time I was escorted out, the soldiers and guards taking liberties to strike me. Once, in my anger, I uttered a loud curse against Rome, and a soldier drew a weapon. Quickly, I gesticulated wildly and uttered nonsense. Seeing I was crazy, the soldier sheathed his sword and gave me the boot.

Sore, I tried my luck outside the city, and although free of soldiers' brutality, I was at risk of passing robbers. To the west lay the trash heap in a valley known as Gehenna. The poorest of the poor were found here, foraging for food and any useful item. Vapors arose, and it was like a scene of hell. "Kentra!" I cried out repeatedly, and even the poor there thought I was crazy.

Ancient rock-cut tombs pierced the valley's walls, and I wondered if she was holed up in one. I called into a few, but there was no answer. At a pool filled with yellow water, a serpent slipped underwater. I was waiting for it to rise when someone grabbed me from behind. There was more than one, and I did not resist. Dragged away with a blindfold placed over my eyes, I was taken to a cave, dark and damp.

Drug yet further down, I saw flickers of light from torches, and was placed down, with someone taking care to bind me. I felt the presence of other men, their eyes trying to discern me. When the blindfold was removed, I saw several men sitting in a rough circle around a fire.

The Sicarii, I realized, seeing their weapons. I started thinking about what story I could tell them. It didn't take long for them to discover that I wasn't a beggar. The man next to me pointed out my undergarment of clean white linen and my well-washed skin.

"Are you a Roman spy?" the man directly asked.

My life depended on my answer, and there was no time to invent fanciful stories. Being caught in a lie could easily mean my death. "I'm a Roman Officer," I replied.

It sounded like my death was at hand from the reaction of the group. Some men grimaced; others flared their teeth. One pulled a knife. The leader held his hand up.

"Who did you come here?" asked a man who seemed their leader.

"The woman named Kentra, a slave woman whom I freed, ran away."

My response surprised the leader. "If you have freed her, why do you seek to find her?"

"She is not well. She needs me."

The leader sensed my story was too unpredicted to smack of falsehood and might be true. He asked for the woman's description and name.

When I told him, a man came forward. "Could it be this is my sister of the same name and age, lost to a slave ship two years ago?"

I gained leave to tell the story in full, and the brother broke down and cried. "It is her for sure," he said.

A debate ensued in their own language, and I gathered it was for my life. The brother argued for me as if I were family.

"There is one question that remains," said the leader. "How was it that you came all the way to Jerusalem for this one woman? Certainly, you had another reason."

"There is more," I admitted, figuring this wouldn't hurt my cause. "I was sent to investigate the Christian cult which worships bones."

"Is it true that you were sent you to investigate them and not us?" asked the leader. "They make poor fighters and fled before the rebellion. We know the empire has a far reach. There is a group west of here."

The group voted, and the thumbs up carried, although a few had voted down as they would not pass up the blood of a Roman officer.

The crazed woman has saved my life, I realized.

Blindfolded again, I was taken a distance from the tomb and released. The light was bedazzling, and when my eyes adjusted, I saw I was alone.

I wandered west, confused. It turned out that Kentra had a connection with assassins.

Dark fell, and I slept under the shelter of a tree. During the night, a hand shook me awake. It was the brother of Kentra again. He led me forward toward a valley, which we reached at the turn of dawn. He pointed below at an encampment. "I believe she is there among them. Protect her."

In my hand he had placed a token. "The protection of the Sicarii," he said, and in the next moment he was gone.

CHAPTER XI

A HEALING

I wondered why the brother was giving her to my charge. Perhaps as a member of assassins he had been forced to leave his family behind. *She is a Christian, after all*, I thought, as I descended the valley. As I neared, I wondered if it would be my final time to see her, and how attached I had become to her. What was my motive? To come and claim her? Wouldn't she be happiest among her own kind, those who understood her?

I didn't enter the camp, for something disturbed me more than the Sicarii. I could not place my finger on it, but it felt like a protective circle around the camp. I returned to Jerusalem for Philo's help.

"What have you learned in that goat-skin?" asked Philo.

"It brings you smacks from soldiers and only shreds of kindness from others except the poorest of poor."

"So, you have become wiser," jested Philo.

"I've learned more." I told the story of my abduction.

Philo was amazed I escaped the Sicarii, and that I hadn't reported the encounter.

"My orders make no mention informing on the Sicarii, and one of them saved my life."

"After meeting an imperial investigator, they'll move their hideout anyway," said Philo. "One thing puzzles me still. Why did the brother show you the Christian camp?"

"Perhaps he's hoping I would take her away from them."

"And why, after escaping the Sicarii, do you fear unarmed Christians?"

"I can't explain it. A fear arose in me. Perhaps if you came with me...."

"Let's go meet the *Mattheans* then. I have not been idle while you are gone. They ready for their feast on the day of the Sun."

"Mattheans, I thought they were in Alexandria?"

"The one named Matthew established the Jerusalem version of this cult. They follow Jewish law strictly and yet claim to be part of this new sect. Their rituals, like the others though, give special recognition to the sun, for they worship on Sunday, which is tomorrow."

"How should we go? I want no more of this goatskin."

"The skin's use is not over. They are unlikely to befriend ones who just destroyed their holy city. I propose we go as cripples at night. We can be Roman outcastes."

That night, my garb required little modification. I added a crutch. Philo, for his part, feigned blindness, and he practiced giving a blank stare that would not blink before a flame.

"What about Kentra?" I asked. "If she's there, she might spot us."

"It is a risk," agreed Philo. "But we first must gain entrance. They might take her for mad, anyway."

At this inopportune time, the centurion of the city entered our tent.

"I was writing a letter to the emperor," he said, staring at us, "and wondered if you would like to report your progress?"

"Tell him we have found the sect and are infiltrating it this very night."

"Should I add the mission goes hard, that you have felt the boot of Rome?"

I looked surprised.

The centurion went on, "One of my soldiers reports colorful curses came Rome's way by a beggar man which matched your look."

"Cursing Rome?" I said defensively. "I am an Imperial Investigator."

The centurion broke out in laughter. "No doubt it was part of your excellent disguise. I'd curse Rome too, if I had to live an hour in that garb. I hope you will make no mention of kicks by my soldiers, and I'll make no mention of your curses. And for tonight, I'll tell my officers to go easy on any beggars that come their way."

The centurion was efficient and more than we deserved. When we walked through the town, the soldiers only eyed us, wary of kicking someone who knew the emperor. The regular beggars sensed something was different too, and boldly strutted about, begging from all.

It was near dawn when we approached the Christian encampment and found they had gathered for their ritual, with incantations and incensing.

I had not reminded Philo about the protective circle, yet he felt it too. "Throw away your crutch," said Philo, suddenly. "We cannot feign illness. They will see through it. We will go in plain robes."

"And if any ask who we are?"

"Let me speak," said Philo. "It will depend on what we find there. Do not show any abnormal reaction to what you see. If people wail, you wail; if people are silent, you are silent. If they cut out a heart, if they castrate themselves, don't show you're appalled. If sexual license occurs, don't reveal your moral qualms lest you be discovered."

Wondering if I had somehow read the group wrong, or if Philo knew more than he let on, I descended toward the group with care. We found them facing the rising sun, veiled by clouds, and singing a hymn. No one asked us questions, and they made space for us.

On a pallet, a woman was lying still, and I wondered if she were dead. Various sayings were read. At times they repeated things in Latin. There must be Romans among the cult. I heard phrases—none inflammatory toward Rome, the closest being a mention of the holy vine of David, perhaps a veiled reference to Kingship.

After more prayers, we joined them for a ritual meal. I wondered if it was a funeral service. The sunlight broke the clouds, and I gained a closer look at the woman on the pallet. It was Kentra. Tears came to my eyes. Was she mortally sick or dead already? I hid my emotion, lest I be discovered.

The meal was part of the ceremony. Bread that was termed body was served. In Latin, they spoke of bread which has been scattered, then gathered as one. My imagination was stimulated, and I wondered if this referred to the Phoenix, in which bread, body and bones were symbolically joined.

Philo was close to the table, inspecting the elements. But we saw no sign of potions or drugs. *Cults often use drugs to heighten religious experience,* he had whispered.

At one point they offered the holy kiss, but it didn't descend into an orgiastic rite. I found myself edging closer to her. I couldn't control myself. I reached out and took her hand. It was conspicuous, and people noticed. Kentra stirred. The group spoke in hushed tones. Philo was disturbed by the chain of events.

The leader of the service came over to Kentra and held her hand. "Do you know this woman?" he asked.

I tried to say no, but I couldn't. I remained silent, but my tears gave me away.

"Even our cures have not succeeded," he said. "Yet she stirred when you touched her. Are you a healer?"

"No."

"You must have some connection to her. She stirred, even now she swoons. She came to us days ago. We have known her, but she has lost her name to give it again."

There was no denying anything now. The woman had unveiled me again. "Her name is Kentra. I brought her to Jerusalem."

"You are a Roman and a slave owner," said the man, his tone surprisingly measured. "Is that why you have sought her out?"

The woman must have already spoken something about me. I could explain that I had freed her too, but that would be too unlikely to be believed. I could not readily explain why I sought her out. Yet the leader's look remained nonjudgmental. It seemed he was only asking these questions to help the woman.

My silence must have convicted me, and bearing the sins of Rome, I waited for the man to speak further.

"Can you pray over her?" he asked.

Surprised, I admitted, "I do not pray to your God."

"Pray in the way you know, but to a God who is above the emperor. There are many stories in our scriptures where God hears the foreigner."

I could not remember the last time I prayed, but I knew I must try. I looked at Philo. Perhaps he knew the right magical incantation, but he kept his head down. No use exposing him. If I failed, what would happen?

I put my hands on her and prayed a childhood prayer to the Father of Gods. Then I took the bone charm off and laid it by her neck, and her face flushed red. She spoke, asking for water. After drinking, she was able to sit up, though dazed. She recognized me and embraced me.

The crowd cried out and raised their hands, "A miracle!"

In the commotion that followed, Philo whispered, "I think we should leave before this gets out of hand and they seek to make us one of their own."

"Is there no more to be gained here?" I asked.

"Unless you want a wife," asked Philo.

We tried to slip away, but several in the group stopped us. "Why do you go?" they asked.

"We are due to go on a voyage," I replied. Philo was walking away, pretending to not know me.

"Will you not stay with her for a time? You have lived with her," said one who I took to be a member of her family.

"I helped her. I freed her from slavery," I said. "I have not had relations with her."

"The bond is strong," said the leader. "She will waste away, if you leave her now."

"I can't...." I said. The faces looked uncomprehending around me. It was true. I had once lived close to her and had returned to give her life. Now I needed to leave. But why then had I come? It looked bad, even to me. "In a year's time, I will return," I promised.

The leader picked up the bone piece and gave to it to me as a seal. "Do not forget your promise."

CHAPTER XII

JAILED IN ANTIOCH

"Where to next?" asked Philo.

"Antioch, the crossroads to the east," I answered. "Undoubtedly, some of the twelve went east, as it is a cult of the rising sun."

Our ship followed the coast of Phoenicia, and Philo pointed out that it was obviously named, ironically, after the Phoenix. Scanning the tops of green-covered mountains, I found myself searching, as if to spy the Phoenix's home. Myth had it her nest lay atop a giant palm.

Memories of Kentra surfaced, and I found myself missing her. The sea was placid; things were too predictable. I fought off a sudden sympathy for the cult.

Sensing my disturbed state of mind, Philo asked what ailed me, but I kept my thoughts close to the vest.

We crossed the River Orantes and reached Antioch, the crown of the Orient and bridge to the east. Its crenelated walls glimmered as they circled a city built atop a flood plain. Yet higher walls of a recently built acropolis marked the governor's palace.

At the South Gate, we were surprised to see a massive, winged creature in gold. "It's one of the cherubim from the temple," said Philo. "The emperor's omen of victory."

"I suppose we should infiltrate the local sect, first." I said. "But how do we do this? It's hard to tell by looking, who's in the cult or not."

"I'll go to the synagogues as a poor tradesman."

"I'll dress the same but wander the streets and see what I can find."

We made a few purchases, and in an inn changed to our new station in life. I wandered most of the day without any result. But in the late afternoon, I came upon a religious fanatic preaching near the town square. Was this one of the twelve?

"After their baptism into me, my disciples do not die," he raved.

One in the crowd called out his name, "Meander!"

I approached after his long oration and asked, "Are you are a Christian?"

"There is only one, and it is I."

"Have you seen any of the twelve?"

"Why be concerned with twelve mortals, when I am he?"

"He is the One!" said someone who looked unsavory.

"The authorities wish to question the twelve. We have only come upon bones and death."

"They will all die!" he hissed. "You only need to find me. I have conquered the angels that created this world! Rome is nothing compared to the power I have."

The man was dangerously inflated, and perhaps he secretly wished Rome would martyr him. But he was too crazy to represent a real threat, I judged, and I doubted if he had any useful intelligence. Still, I took my chances and asked if he knew the whereabouts of a Christian house. Meander wasn't above betraying his competition and signaled a follower to show me.

The slave appeared deaf and dumb, and I followed him into the city. *Could it be a trap?* I wondered. But the slave man left after pointing out a house, and I stood watch into the early evening. Nothing seemed out of the ordinary. *Had I been sent on a fool's errand?*

But late evening––the group was given to nocturnal events––the house revealed itself as a place of gathering by the number of people who entered there. They the usual varied types from laborers to lettered Greeks, and again I sensed such diverse bonds could represent a threat. I tried to discern who might be their leader of those who came, but there were no symbols of authority. Or perhaps their leader was already inside, the owner of the house.

I knocked on the door and was allowed in without comment. The people's friendly visages surprised me, and the array of people which included a Roman soldier. Fortunately, my sailor's habits helped me to fit in. I told them the truth in part, that I heard disparaging words about them from Meander and wanted to see for myself what they were about.

"Welcome," said a woman who looked as if she had been tasked as a greeter. "We are all friends, joined by the Risen One."

People shared about their lives, and someone asked me, and I was able to bring my recent sailing days into conversation and share lively stories from the high sea. Although I enjoyed their company, I warned myself to be careful and not fall under their spell. I began to wonder if this was the same group who did rituals with bones when a commotion started. Several soldiers with drawn swords were entering the house. We were caught in one of the governor's dragnets.

When I tried to tell an officer that I was a Roman citizen on a mission from the emperor, he laughed. All of us were ushered through the streets to a holding cell. The Christian group was now mixed with criminals and lesser rouges and vagabonds.

I demanded to speak to the jailor, but I could only yell out. "I have imperial orders. I am a friend of the emperor!" Both jailers and prisoners took me for mad. I raved and banged against the bars until the jailor threatened me with ten lashes. The brothers and sisters from the cult put their arms around me and tried to settle me down.

"I am a special emissary of the emperor," I protested. "I'm not a member of this cult. I've been sent to investigate."

The jailer, who overheard, mocked, "The Bone Investigator. Tell that to the judge." Afterwards, he tossed leftover bones from his meal my way.

Despite my revelation, the group still treated me well, even offering me portions of their meal. One in particular watched over me, a young man named Mathias.

"It's true," I said. "I'm searching for the twelve, before they become bones."

"All men will become bones," he answered. "But one day the faithful will rise."

"We're both mad then," I admitted. "Me, for paying this any mind, and you for your belief."

Later that evening a large, muscled vagabond tried to take my shoes, but Mathias stopped him. The far lesser in size, his unshakeable bearing caused the giant to back down.

"When I get out of here, I owe you," I said.

"I will pray for you," said the man. "Your mission puts you at risk."

The next day we were dragged up to the acropolis. Word had spread, and angry citizens pelted us with small stones.

A familiar face greeted me in the square. "Philo! How did you find me?"

"I heard the soldier's gossip about having arrested a bone investigator."

Philo showed the surprised soldiers our documents, and I was immediately released.

"Quick, change of venue," said Philo. "We are due to see the Governor."

In a brief space, I had changed from a prisoner facing charges to an emissary of the emperor.

"They're troublesome," the Governor said, half in apology for my treatment. "They disregard our customs. They don't sacrifice to the emperor, nor go to the circus or our baths! The mix the order of things. I've had too many complaints."

"The emperor is concerned too," I said. "But my mission is to locate the twelve."

"Yes, their leaders ... They come and go like the wind, usually one step ahead of us." The Governor then showed me one of their cups with crude artwork. "Six persons in the east and six in the west. You go to Antioch, then they're in Edessa."

"Some have died, already," I revealed.

"They'll simply replace them," said the Governor. "There is one here, a certain Mathias."

I was surprised to hear the name, and wondered it was the same man who helped me. Would he have given kindness to his enemy?

"He is said to replace one who betrayed their leader," the Governor went on. "His activity has proved particularly irksome, and I would not be bothered if he were to die. I believe that I should send out orders to that effect now. I will have the group arrested this day checked out."

The governor's words explained why Matthias was not on the original list of 12 but talk of his impending death shocked me. A man who had helped a Roman could not be a real threat to Rome. Plus, if the oracle was true, a dead Mathias was not in the emperor's interest.

"There is a certain Mathias, a young man—certainly not the one you speak of—who is among a group with which I was just imprisoned. He is an important connection here in Antioch and will it serve the emperor to free him."

"Did the emperor send you here to free my prisoners?" asked the Governor with a note of irritation in his voice. "No matter ... if the emperor can be helped.... This group is more bothersome than not, and there are more violent ones to worry about. I will release them all if you wish."

"You have our thanks," I replied.

The Governor readily passed on the orders. No doubt Mathias and his group would attribute their release to their God.

"I'm disturbed by this replacement principle," I told Philo afterwards. "Maybe the *twelve* never really die, by simply replacing themselves. The threat they pose may develop in the future, past our lives."

"Perhaps," granted Philo. "But so far, I must admit, we've seen little threat. Maybe it's enemies they engender that we should worry about, like Meander."

"Orders are orders," I said. "Besides, I don't think we have penetrated the full mystery yet. What do you suggest we do next? Question Mathias further?"

"There is another possibility—mediums."

Philo went on to answer my questioning look. "They consult the dead. Perhaps we can put your bone to another use."

CHAPTER XIII

THE BONE AND THE GHOST

There were many reasons to go to Edessa. Not only was it the eastern outpost of the Empire, but six of the twelve had indeed gone east, according to the Governor. It was also rumored that the leader's burial cloth had been secreted there. Last, Philo believed mediums would be more plentiful there.

We traveled in a lightweight carriage following the King's road. Along the way I fell into reverie, a lucid dreaming. I was returning triumphantly to Rome, bringing back the Phoenix bird itself. It had died but did not decay. We were to give it an imperial funeral, but a discussion arose about how to dispose of the remains. Certainly, we could not burn it, lest it rise again. We decided to entomb it deep within a stone mausoleum, but only after we dismembered it. "Cut it up," ordered the emperor, but as they came to the twelfth piece, I shouted "No!" It was too late, for the bird rose, its plumage spread to gigantic size, and its florid red beak dove into the emperor's neck.

I awoke in a hot sweat and told my dream to Philo. "We must be careful," he said. "Whether we bring back news of the twelve alive or dead."

After a week of travel, we arrived in Edessa and found but faint signs of Christian presence. People looked at us puzzled and askance when we asked about a burial cloth. One man, seeking to make money, showed us winding sheets that held an impress of the dead. But there was no aroma or any sign to indicate it was from the Bone Cult.

None of our usual tricks worked. I dressed as a beggar, Philo as a scholar, but not a clue surfaced. The governor dismissed our concerns, saying there are many mystery cults and that he doesn't bother with them unless a Roman was killed.

"Perhaps, it is time to consult the world beyond," Philo suggested. "Meander gave me a name."

"Isn't that risky? I have heard stories...."

Philo agreed in part. "The dead are unpredictable, but their power in the world of the living is limited."

"How do we call upon one?"

"We have a bone from one of the twelve. The medium will know what to do from there."

It did not take long to find one, for we were willing to pay well. I had imagined an elderly widow in a dark part of the city, seeking money for survival, but Philo secured a soothsayer in the upper, well-to-do city quarter. A short, stocky man dressed in an elaborate robe greeted us, and we were ushered into a darkened room, where only muffled noises penetrated from the outside.

"Interesting," said the medium after listening to our story. "You want me to conjure someone who has been violently executed by the state. Would not such a spirit be hostile, and especially to highly placed officials of Rome?"

I had made no mention of our rank to the woman, so I took this as a sign of her authenticity.

I dropped the pretense and informed her of our purpose.

She went on to say. "This new group, although they do not keep all the Roman customs, do not advocate revolt or violence against Rome. Perhaps the emperor should task his best minds elsewhere."

The woman was shrewd, giving compliments. But I did not let it deter me from the task at hand.

I held up the polished bone, which even in the faint light seemed to have an uncanny glow. "Perhaps you can help us to contact one of his original followers. The one to whom this bone belonged."

The medium took the bone from me and examined it closely. "Yes, this relic is highly charged, and you have stolen it. Do you know how he died?"

"I do not know much about his execution. I had heard that he was only beheaded, treated as a Roman citizen. Can you help us or not? We deal with any threats upon the Roman state—whether from the dead or living."

"Yes, threats come from all directions.... This is a powerful spirit, and I would expect an appropriate sum of money and a small gift."

"What sort of gift?" asked Philo, wondering what that was about.

"A simple possession you carry with you."

"Then summon the spirit and we will grant your request," I directed.

"To be fair, I must warn that I do not know how this spirit will react to being summoned. It may instantly leave, or it may stay and incur some harm. I would still expect to be paid."

"Do it," I said. "We want to ask if their phoenix is due to arise, and if so, how he may be stopped."

The medium did not seem surprised at my reference, nor query me as to what I meant. She called upon the spirit. It took time, with abundant incense and incantations, the room filling with smoke. The first change we noticed was that we felt light, as if floating on clouds from underneath us. Then a pervading darkness covered us, as if we were deep within the earth. A form took shape, surrounded by light, though its face was obscured.

"You disturb me from important matters," said the spirit.

"The Roman emperor has--"

"I do not answer to trivial powers," the spirit interrupted.

"We seek the twelve who followed the Crucified One."

At that the darkness revealed a more human form, a handsome man in a scarlet red robe.

Philo and I were amazed. "What is your name?" we asked.

"You ask my name? Is that why you have summoned me? Call me Metastasis."

"We are searching for a body," Philo informed.

"Bodies can be found, but your request is a matter of spirit," the ghost instructed. "But if you are interested in bodies, come closer and look."

From within his cloak, he pulled out a tiny book. The pictures moved and appeared to come alive as we saw them. There were scenes of a man who taught crowds, healed, and was cruelly executed. The last scene showed a tomb, then utter dark. "It's quite senseless," said Metastasis. "Some do good, others evil. But all come to the same end."

"Will Rome be conquered by this man's followers?" I asked bluntly.

"Why worry about the fate of Rome," he said, showing another set of pictures. In it, Rome was burning and overrun by people in alien dress. "Yes, these call themselves Christians, a recent persuasion."

"So, it is true!" exclaimed Philo.

"Is there no way to stop them?" I asked.

"There is a way," Metastasis replied, and the ghost asked for our relic bone.

I hesitated. I realized that the bone was something I had become attached to, for it had accompanied me on much of my journey and helped to heal Kentra. Then too, I was safekeeping the relic, to bring it back to her. I hesitated, as Philo looked at me, wondering why I delayed.

The spirit darkened. Then neared me and spoke again. "Yes, there is a way to stop them. See!"

In my hand, the bone changed. It became a flesh decaying and shriveled into something black and burnt. Then it turned back to its white polished form, but the prior image was seared into my mind.

"You see now what you really have," said ghost. "I can take it off your hands."

But I saw this was no longer possible. The bone-flesh felt merged with my hand. I stood aghast and puzzled, for the bone appeared to have the power to make my own flesh decay. Yet, it could also transform back to the living bone....

It led me to distrust the spirit, for it smacked of the dark arts. And I gathered that he was trying to take something valuable from me. I closed my hand upon this bone, which had this power of transformation. He would have to take my hand, to take it away from me.

The room changed, and we were in another place. The spirit was still asking for the bone, but its aspect had become huge, frightening. The bone was no longer joined to my flesh. It was a bone again, but glowing. It was burning my hand, causing intense pain. Still, I did not drop it, so that the ghost could take it. For then--I suddenly sensed--the apparition could become real. I do not know how long the pain lasted, nor how I could have held out so long. All the way, I kept thinking of Kentra, that she would need me to return.

Then I was back again in the room of the medium, the bone still in my hand.

The medium held surprise in her face that it was still in my possession.

"Do you not want to destroy the cult?" she asked.

I answered, "The spirit I encountered was not concerned with Rome or her enemies." With that, we paid the woman her sum of money and prepared to leave. The medium, however, did not forget to ask for the simple gift. "Your focale, please."

The sweat cloth which I wore around my neck and kept from my soldiering days had sentimental value, but it could be replaced. I handed it over.

"We are even now," I asked, not wanting to leave her dissatisfied.

"We are, but not so with the spirit. You have made an enemy more deadly than the first."

CHAPTER XIV

LETTERS

That same evening I wrote a letter to the emperor, reporting on the investigation's progress. I had been left disturbed by the seance, coming away with the knowledge that there were indeed other powerful forces besides Rome. I also bothered by having left a possession with the medium and to what purpose she might turn that toward. I became convinced that these matters needed more help from a ritual specialist beyond what Philo provided. Here reads the text:

"The Phoenix cult is flourishing in at least three major cities of the empire. The twelve have thus far largely eluded us, going to extremities of east and west. Two, perhaps three have turned to bones already, and we've had no success in locating any live apostles, except for one who shortly died after our visit and recently a replacement one named Matthias.

As for the Phoenix itself, this Son of Man, there are prophecies that one day he will appear in the sky and raise an army of the dead at the sound of a trumpet. No trace of his remains has been found. We did contact a spirit of the dead who promised help, but further contact will be risky without more assistance. Although we have found no overt disloyalty to Rome with this cult, except for a few mad ravings, we also find not all the usual loyalties. It is by their writings that they promise this Phoenix-man will one day return and Rome will mysteriously dissolve. They think this will happen soon. On one level these fantastic saying and beliefs do not threaten Rome. The cult bears no arms nor has any plans to do violence directly against Rome. Yet, and Philo agrees, there is something un-Roman about them that would undermine Rome from within. They are not really Roman but members of the Cult of Bones, tapping into their dark powers to heal the possessed and sick, and thereby gain a following.

The usual methods to stamp out such a group will not work. For persecution and execution simply creates more bones, more fuel for their cause. Even if we burn them or deposit them in the sea, I suspect they would use pieces of cloth that they touched. We had rumor about an image found on a cloth....

"I suggest we end the search and let this cult come to its own fantastical end. It will no doubt play out, for every fantasy has its limits. We await your word."

Philo disagreed with my decision not to pursue more apostles. We had intelligence that a certain Nathaniel had been in Babylon.

"There are only ruins there," I said.

"Among ruins and ashes, a Phoenix may be nesting," countered Philo.

"I think you would be intrigued to meet the Babylonian seers. But we are not here to satisfy your curiosity but to serve the emperor."

Philo tried a different tack. "The spirit of the dead suggested we are dealing with powerful spiritual forces. We may need the wisdom of the east to guide our way."

I wondered if this was the solution I had been seeking in my letter to the emperor. Could we task a Babylonian ritual expert to help our cause?

Philo waited for this moment to yield his best hand, "You did not give up the bone."

"I did not trust the spirit," I said. "Besides, it held no loyalty to Rome."

"Do you expect a spirit to be concerned with political powers?"

"No. But there was still something I didn't like about it."

"Perhaps you've come to believe that bone holds some power," said Philo.

"I am not superstitious. It's a memento, a little thing to remind me of the slave girl, that's all!"

Philo did not believe me. I wondered if he would file an independent letter of his own, favoring the investigation to continue. Perhaps, too, he felt I was becoming one of them, revealing the true danger of the cult.

While we awaited word, a letter from the emperor crossed paths. He ordered us to continue the search for the 12 at all costs. "Let nothing deter you," it read. He reported a dream his wife had. An arrow had pierced the Phoenix's breast, and it appeared that Rome would be safe. But instead of safety, twelve small chicks hungrily fed on the blood, and she could see them growing before her eyes.

I had no choice. Even if with the letter expressing my doubts, I knew what his answer would be. "On to Babylon," I said.

CHAPTER XV

CRYSTAL TOMB

Going East meant leaving the Roman empire and an armed escort. We disguised ourselves ahead of time as Pearl merchants, wearing turbans, and acquired a skiff to head south on a tributary down to the Euphrates. The stream, still filled from the winter rains, cut a narrow course through a limestone plateau. On the right we could see the Arabian desert.

"Stories had it that the Phoenix was born here," said Philo. I surveyed the cliffs expectantly and spotted a golden eagle's nest atop a cliff. Downy feathers and fresh green sprays showed it to be a live nest.

We stopped below for the night and the next morning, on a whim, I ascended to inspect the nest. The mother eagle circled wide overhead but appeared distantly curious. The nest was incredibly large, over ten feet wide. Two flightless, white downy eaglets squawked within. Bones of prey and twigs intertwined. I was readying to leave, then noticed the thinness of one of the eaglets. Knowing that the smaller eaglet would die, I hooded the creature with a strip of cloth. Its awful screams sent its mother diving.

Quickly, I left the nest with the eaglet in hand. The eagle made a single pass as I brandished a knife, but settled upon its nest, content to find its prize young still there.

"Eagle snatching!" said Philo upon my return.

"He's the runt," I said. "He would have died, anyway."

"Perhaps you will learn more of the Phoenix's habits."

"I wonder if the myth started with the eagle. The same nest used for hundreds of years, becoming huge, with bones of prey mixed in. There was an aroma too from the evergreens."

The eaglet provided a diversion for our trip. We fed it fish from the river, and rabbit meat on our camping stops. Eventually, the eaglet grew large enough to fly and one morning, she disappeared.

On one of our stops, we came upon Persian travelers, who we exchanged stories and told about our search for the Phoenix. "Ancient fallen gods lay buried in the ruins," they said of Babylon. The eldest among them spoke about a deathless chieftain, immortal in the flesh, who would rise and fight one day. These events occurred in a great millennia cycle, and it struck me as a version of the Phoenix myth.

Within a couple hundred miles from Babylon, the landscape dramatically changed. The land became flat and crisscrossed with ancient canals. We had come to the Land of Two Rivers, with layers of alluvial soil that brought fertility atop the thin white crusts of salt. The river slowed and broadened, and we drifted on to Babylon.

The city was still populated, but the ancient portion lay in ruins. A sizeable Jewish community was here from days when the Assyrians deported large populations. The Jews here did not support the revolt in Jerusalem.

We were drawn to ancient Babylon, its fortifications largely intact, and its palaces and temples half standing. "An ideal site for clandestine meeting grounds," I surmised.

We walked through the ancient King's palace several hundred years distant and came upon a half-finished basalt figure of a lion trampling a man. In the center of the ruins stood a more recent Parthian palace where its Kings collected statues of gods in a vast hall. There were no guards at the entrance, and the crouched figure of a broken lion offered no resistant. Many of the god statues lay about, broken. "One wonders if Rome's gods will meet the same fate one day," I said.

The inner recesses of the palace were topped by a dome-like edifice that defied architectural expectation, and we wondered at its origin. Underneath it, a stone platform held an impossibly large stone crystal the size of a small boat. We were amazed at the stone's size and that it had not been plundered. When we came up to it, we saw, to our amazement, that a body lay within, white robed and bearded. The crystal magnified things, so the body appeared larger than its normal size. We spoke in half tones as we gazed. The expression on the man's face did not look like death, but as if he was in a deep sleep. Around the head, a light flickered, and I realized it must be scattered reflections from the crystal. I touched the stone, half expecting it to flash.

"Could this be our Phoenix?" I ventured to ask.

"No crucified markings," said Philo. "But there is a red hue in the garment around his chest."

"Perhaps he was stabbed to death."

"There is mystery here," said Philo. "How could the body be placed within a rock crystal?"

"We could ask him?" I jested.

A ray of light broke through from above and flickered into colors. Philo said, "We may not need a medium."

"This spirit seems more aggregable than the one the medium summoned," I said.

"If he is one of the twelve," said Philo. "Then the prophecy will not be fulfilled. He is frozen in time and will not change into bones."

"So, we have won. We only need to secure this body or somehow take it back."

"We would have to bring the crystal too, for I think the body would decay if we took it out."

"Moving it would challenge the builders of the pyramid; it would require a cohort of men and expert handlers."

"Perhaps the body only needs to be guarded."

"Someone else is doing that already," I said. "There's no dust on the stone."

"Perhaps the energy from the crystal takes care of this," Philo speculated.

We resolved to stay the night and the next day to see if anyone would come. During the night, our fire caused refractions in the rock crystal, which appeared to dance as sparks beyond what they should.

"I have an eerie feeling," reported Philo. "That we will not have to call upon the spirits this night for them to come."

CHAPTER XVI

CRACKED CRYSTAL

It was thus that I met a spirit, if spirit it was, and one who had an undecayed body. I do not know whether I called it forth, or whether it came of its own. The night had become ominous as the crystal appeared to come under attack by a dark force. It was attempting to break through a protective shield that included us, and I called to the body that lay within. "Save us from whatever threatens us!"

The body glowed––I don't know whether this was in my dream or not––and a light projected out of the crystal case.

The darkness fled, but a new fear pervaded me: Had I conjured a ghost, an enemy of Rome. Confused, I asked the spirit, "Will you help Rome?"

"My cause is not earthly kingdoms," the spirit of the body said.

"But there is much good to Rome."

Then appearing within the crystal on its sides were scenes that flitted as if projected from the case. It showed life in Rome, starting with houses along the river, but then it went deeper ... into slave mines, galleys, and slaves crucified. It was as if I felt their pain. "Stop!" I cried. The screen shifted to the lives of the nobility, the vomitorium, their cruel entertainments in the arenas, and I saw that they too were slaves in a different way.

Then the spirit faded, and I fell into an exhausted sleep.

Philo woke me that morning, but I was tired, as if I had not slept. Philo listened with interest to my "dream." Although I insisted it was a vision, he said that it was more likely a dream, for I knew not the art of conjuring spirits.

"It appeared after my request for help," I informed.

"That would be new," said Philo. "Spirits summoned by a simple wish. Or perhaps, this cult has succeeded in trapping the dead in a new way which makes them more accessible."

"Are you saying that he is still alive in there?"

"Yes. Kept alive by the energy of the crystal. You can feel its vibration when you lay your hands on the case."

I placed my hands on the case and felt nothing at first. Then my hands tingled with warmth and a faint light shone through them.

I startled, hearing steps. A man of large height and wearing a white robe had entered the chamber. For a moment I thought the spirit had returned, but Philo, who recognized the white girdle cord, said he was a priest of Zoroaster.

The Magi went directly to the crystal case and stared within. "Are you tending the coffin now?" he asked.

"We are seekers," Philo answered. "We wonder what mystery this is."

The priest cast a sidelong glance at us. "The body has moved again," he noted.

"Do you not fear contamination?" said Philo. "I have heard that those of your country burn the dead."

"This one is encased in pure crystal," said the priest. "And there are some who do not bring death's curse. In ancient times, our own kings were embalmed and placed in living rock. And this crystal is from the very vault of heaven."

"Who lies within?" I queried.

The answer was enigmatic. "One of the deathless chieftains, immortal in the flesh. One day he will rise among others and fight against our enemies."

"The spirit said is not concerned with the survival of earthly kingdoms," I said.

"There is only one true kingdom."

"Is he not one of the twelve who vies against Rome?"

"Have you not had words with him?" asked the priest. "He will not remain encased here forever." The Persian then made offerings of water, and lighting a bowl of incense, offered fire. After a lengthy petition, he left.

We spent the rest of the day contemplating events and surveying the surrounding ruins. "Here was one of the twelve," I finally concluded. "Though unnamed."

"Or perhaps the Phoenix itself," said Philo.

"We still face the same question. How can we stop the dead who still live? Can we kill it twice?"

"This rock crystal will make a second blow harder," Philo replied. "The only thing to do, is to continue our vigil. Perhaps the spirit itself will tell us the answer."

"What of the darkness that came? I worry about that."

"Yes, that is our true enemy," Philo discerned.

The vigil extended for several days and went by peacefully. Each day, the Magi reappeared. It knew more than we but was not forthcoming in his knowledge. Still, he encouraged our watch.

One week after its first appearance, the darkness came again, this time thicker and stronger. It took shape above the coffin and appeared as a spirit ten times darker and fouler than it was before. Our faces blanched; our eyes burned at the sight.

The spirit laughed and reached with its elongated hands, lifting the crystal coffin with ease. It was set to destroy the body. "No!" I cried, rushing forward.

The dark spirit raised a finger, causing me to freeze, an incredible pressure bearing on me.

Suddenly another spirit, a luminous being rent the darkness with a sword of light. A mortal combat ensued over the crystal case and the body within.

The shock of combat was too great. We felt our bodies loosen as a bright lance of light crossed the dark. We lapsed into unconsciousness.

When we woke at dawn, we rushed to the case. The Persian Magi was already there. The crystal case had been cracked, and there was no trace of the body. Seared marks were around, the crystal burned and blackened. Fractured shards lay scattered around. We told the Magi what we had witnessed.

"It is strange," he finally said. "He has gone on above, when I thought he would stay for centuries more."

"Do you know his name? Was he one of the twelve?"

"He was called Jude," the Magi revealed. "He came with another from the North, but his companion was taken, his skin flayed. He himself had his heart pierced."

"They are the last, then?" I wondered. "Have all the twelve died?"

"I have heard that one has gone to the far east, to the land of peacocks."

"Then our journey next takes us there," I said.

"I don't know why you go to such lengths," said the Magi. "But take this as a memory of your vigil." He gave us an inner piece of the crystal which had adjoined the body. It was tetrahedral, faultless except for a crack that looked like a lens in the middle. I tried to look through it, as if to see my future. But the crack held a darkness that would not reveal itself.

CHAPTER XVII

A BRAHMIN IN THE FOREST

We bordered a merchant ship leaving down the lower Euphrates, past white encrusted fields. Evaporation of sea water had left the layers of salt, causing infertility that hastened Babylon's decline. We stopped at the seaport Eridu for provisions, claiming to be the world's oldest city. At the border of the Roman empire, we refreshed our disguise as Pearl merchants and banded with a group of travelers seeking spices in India. The ship made haste, following the direct route over the open sea. The discovery of the monsoon wind, the *Hippalus* freed us from the tedious necessity to hug the coast. Our destination was a Roman merchant community named Arikkamedu in Southern India.

Most aboard the ship were merchants seeking India's spices and pearls. One of the band seemed strangely removed, with whom Philo and I started a conversation. We mentioned our journeys through the great cities of Alexandria, Jerusalem, and Antioch.

The man was not impressed and broke his silence. "He who understands the world, has found only a corpse."

From then on, he would grant an enigmatic sentence every so often. He said that he too was seeking pearls, although of a different type. When I asked his origin, he replied, "We come from the light."

Philo said he sounds like one of the "Knowers," a sect who believed they had secret knowledge that delivered them from the world.

The man also left tantalizing clues that he knew about the Phoenix Cult. When we told him of our encounters with prophets along our journey, he said, "You have mentioned the dead and leave out the Living One."

The ship's Triarch knew that his name was Didymos, and that he was a religious fanatic of an obscure sect. "It is best to leave such alone," he warned, "lest they place a curse on you."

I persisted in talking to him, however, and my persistence was rewarded as we gained his friendship and information about a cult which Philo didn't know. We were near the end of our weeks long journey when he answered a query about the mysterious kingdom.

"It's like a certain man who wanted to kill a powerful man," he related. "In his own house, he draws out his sword and thrusts it through the wall, to see if he has the power to do it. Then he slays the powerful man."

The violent imagery surprised me. *Was the cult a secret school of assassins? What group did he really belong to?* We resolved to follow him upon our landing.

As we came to port, the press of heat hit us, animal smells, and a colorful array of people. We would have quickly lost our man, but Philo asked where he was heading. "Kerala," he said, for once avoiding an enigmatic response.

Kerala was composed largely of traders from various lands. We told Didymos that promised well for our own business, and he agreed to let us accompany him.

It was as good a lead as any we had, and we arrived after an overland voyage of a few days. The land was exotic, tropical, and we saw peacocks in the countryside.

Our guide showed us lodgings at an inn and prepared to go on his way. Philo asked where was going, and Didymos replied, "The shrine in Mylapore."

"We are seekers too," said Philo. "May we come?"

"I will come back for you," he said.

We let him go; it would be too obvious to follow him. He did not return that night, nor the following morning. "We're on our own now," said Philo.

We started asking questions that morning at breakfast. The owner, who spoke our tongue, made short shrift of the temples at Mylapore, but said more exotic temples could be found further up the coast. They were cut in rock, and in the apses were raised Stupamounds, holding the remains of holy men. Groups of disciples worshiped around them.

Has the Phoenix Cult spread this far all already? I couldn't help wondering.

When I asked the name of the cult, the owner informed, "They are followers of Buddha."

Philo had heard of the group but didn't know more than their leader practiced deep meditation and led a life of non-action. "Not likely to be related to the Phoenix cult, for the Apostles are proselytizers and seafarers. Yet in this matter of relics, they are strikingly similar."

The owner said, if we wished to know more, to go into the outlying forest where students of the *Brahmin* live.

It was shortly after breakfast that Didymos reappeared. We were surprised that he had kept his word. We mentioned our project to see the men of the forest, and he agreed to accompany us, saying he had a brother among them.

After a long hike, we came to a thick forest with small, rushing streams. Along its banks, persons were spaced out, still in deep mediation, and we did not interrupt. They wore red undergarments with a black animal skin over top, and their frames were thin from fasting.

"Will they talk to us?" asked Philo.

"The advanced ones will not," Didymos replied.

We came to a young man washing in a stream. His hair was long and unkempt, and he wore only a loin cloth. When we came up to his small encampment unannounced, he showed no surprise. "Have you seen Antaro?" asked Didymos.

The man took a breath, as if he had been suppressing it. "Not for a year. He's deep in the forest, wears no clothes and takes only green food. He talks not."

"Ask this Brahmin if he's heard of a bird that dies and rises again."

Didymos translated his response. "Yes, we know of her. We seek to become her embryos. We dry ourselves and build heat so that we may be reborn as Brahmin. If we were birds, we cast off our feathers, and if we were snakes, our scales."

We departed and Philo surmised, "His saying sounds like he is an adherent of the Phoenix cult. Strange that we have gone so far and find the heart of things."

"No matter," I replied. "Rome is not threatened by those wasting away in the forest."

"No, but my guess is that threaten the powers here," rejoined Philo.

I wondered what he saw that I did not. But I did not ask, for if this was true, what hope had Rome?

CHAPTER XVIII

FIELD OF PEACOCKS

We proceeded through farmland over a dusty road. Monuments to the deified dead dotted the countryside. Mylapore was the City of Peacocks, and along the way the first peacock we saw was dazzling; The blues and greens shined iridescent, as if its eyes-shapes were alive.

We entered the town, merging with the mass of people, their huts openly viewing their household activities: haircutting, cooking, and working their wares. But we entered only to be sent back to the outskirts. Didymos took us quickly through and pointed us toward an outlying field. "The Apostle is known to be there," they say, "effecting cures."

At this point he took his leave to find his own group. The field was populated with peacocks and didn't fly off, but merely shuffled aside as we passed.

"They are half-tamed," Philo commented.

In the field, we spied a lone wayside shrine for one of the deified dead. Inscribed on an upright stone was a cult sign and a peacock. "Our man has already passed," announced Philo.

"Not so long ago," I observed. "The ground is recently upturned, and the flowers are fresh."

"Again, they have beaten us," reflected Philo. "Already turning to bones...."

We sat by a tree near the grave. The heat and smells of fields lulled us to sleep. I dreamed of a man praying, his robe shimmering in light. A long spear lay at his side. "They came hunting for peacocks and slew me," said the man.

"Why would they slay a beautiful bird?" I asked. Blood smeared my hands as I picked up the spear.

The dream was so real that when I woke, I was staring at my hands. "I felt guilty, like I was the one who killed him," I told Philo, who was uncomprehending.

"You look like you're still waking, still seeing the dream," he observed.

"I dreamed of the man, his blood. I held the spear."

"This field is haunted. It must have been a violent death."

"The man's visage looked at peace—he shone."

"But your body was jerking like you were having a seizure," Philo revealed. "I suggest we go. There is something here I don't understand. A violent death doesn't normally receive a wayside shrine."

"Perhaps, it's not surprising. This cult breaks customs everywhere."

When we rose, we noticed a peacock nearby, staring at us. He was of giant size, its feathers a bright coppery sheen.

"Amazing, it shows no fear of us," I whispered. "And its eyes have a human glint."

Somehow, the creature communicated. I sensed meaning, but it eluded me.

The peacock flew off, leaving behind a feather that shone metallic. I picked it up, saying, "Not quite a bone...."

Philo and I walked back to the City of Mylapore, talking over the strange series of events. We decided to investigate the manner of the man's death.

In town we learned that the apostle's name was Thomas, and that he had died within the month. Rumors circulated as to the cause of his sudden death. Some said it was an assassin from the Brahmin class who felt their power threatened. This was despite an official authorization for the Christian community to exist. We had seen it inscribed on a copper plate.

"Could the sect of Didymos be the source of the strongman story?" I speculated.

"He may have been allied with them, but kept it to himself, sensing our motives.

Philo offered other information. "Suspicion might also fall upon a hunting warrior tribe from the Hindu. Their lord of the hunt, named Murkan, had the lance as a weapon. His color was red and his bird the peacock. Their god was one of the sun and eternal youth. Perhaps, they were threatened by the Christian cult."

"They just as well might have joined them," I said.

We heard multiple stories of the man's life, many already embellished with legend. One story bore a startling resemblance to the strange events in the field. A hunter sought the most handsome peacock among a flock and wounded it. The rest flew up, but this peacock turned into man upon dying. It was the apostle....

"Perhaps we saw the apostle after all," I jested with Philo. "We even have a piece of him," I added, waving the feather.

Philo was silent. Perhaps he believed it.

There was nothing more to be found. Once more, we infiltrated a house meeting, but it was the same. They shared bread and wine, ate a meal, sang songs, and recited prayer. Nothing more. "We've come a long way to see a few peacocks and hear some songs," I said.

"There is still a riddle here," said Philo. "I wonder if we are among powerful magicians who can shape shift."

I looked hard at Philo and saw he was seriously considering this. "What grand power would that be, to become a peacock?" I asked. "and even if it were so, how could that threaten Rome?"

"The power to shape-shift would be immense for a spy," Philo considered. "We would not be able to find them, much less kill them. The man becomes a peacock, then a man, then back to a bird again. Maybe the leader of the Bone Cult changed to a Phoenix, then came alive as a man again."

"Fancies," I dismissed. "What amazes me are the rapid inroads they've made, and so far away. Perhaps, it's time to report back in person to the emperor."

"When we only have a few stories and items to share––a whitened bone and a peacock feather? He'll think we're mad. We'll need to bring back a live witness."

"Perhaps someone from Kentra's group would go with us," I said. "But the only one likely to come is Kentra."

"She ever returns to your mind," said Philo. "If I were a prophet, I'd say she'll be accompanying you to the emperor's throne."

CHAPTER XIX

A TRAP AMONG THE TOMBS

The return trip took us through the Red Sea to Alexandria. We only tarried long enough to gain passage on a trireme to Jerusalem. On the voyage, Philo and I took stock of the situation. We had, not surprisingly, failed in stopping the apostles from becoming bones. We had found just half of them, and we had to go to the ends of the earth to do that. Chances are that the other half, for which we had even fewer leads, were already in their resting ground. Our best hope––despite instructions from the emperor's letter––was to follow the Delphic oracle, for finding the bones of the crucified would cause the Phoenix to sleep a thousand more.

It was our last card to play before we reported back. If we had not found one of the twelve living, we had could still find the founder's bones and discredit the cult's claim. Further, if there was magic associated with the bones, in which the cult invoked his ghost, the confiscation of his bones would put a stop to their ritual. It seemed desperate to seek the bones of someone who had died several decades ago. In this connection, the face of Kentra kept coming to mind, and I wondered if she could help us.

As we neared Jerusalem, having traveled a great distance overland, Philo became taciturn, and I had a profound melancholy. Obviously, the bones would be either have disappeared or be well hidden. What clues could be left? We would have to penetrate the sect's innermost circle, something that couldn't be done without feigning conversion. Philo and I discussed this possibility at length, but we felt it would take too much time. Initiation rites typically required a year at a minimum.

On the outskirts of Jerusalem, we found no traces of Kentra's group, as we had hoped they might have returned. They remained somewhere further east, with no more definite word. My depression redoubled at hearing this, that our living link to the cult was gone. A longing for the companionship of a woman came to me.

We made one last stab, hoping to find the burial plot of the founder. No one in any official capacity remembered or would tell us of events 70 years prior. We tried again to query hermits and beggars who saw and remembered much. After many entreaties, a man led us to an abandoned quarry. Cast away limestone blocks littered the ground, their age testifying that it had been centuries since the mine was used. But upon this hill, the man told us, was the place of crucifixion within full view of the city.

Somewhere nearby, the bodies would have been deposited. Tombs should be undisturbed by edict of the emperor, although this wouldn't stop determined cult members or tomb robbers. Our information had it that he was buried with no more than a winding cloth.

Our guide led us to the northern slope and several rock-cut tombs. Apparently, he had knowledge of a specific tomb and pointed it out. Although I did not know whether his claim was accurate, I paid him his gold. The tomb was of good size and not of very ancient age.

We stepped inside. It was remarkably clean—not only unused, but as if someone had been occupying and putting the tomb to use.

"Even stray rocks had been picked up," I noticed.

"The very absence of evidence is evidence," said Philo,

"Someone is using it, but for what?"

Philo was silent. Inside, we saw a handprint in the dust atop a limestone slab where bodies would be laid before removing them to an inner recess. But that print could be from anyone, for any reason.

If there were any other clues, they had long since disappeared.

"The absence heightens the mystery," repeated Philo. "The body must have lain here only a short time before it was secreted away. But it remains a sacred site."

We looked for graffiti. At first we didn't see any, but as a grazing light shifted, faint incised markings came into view. Two were Greek letters, alpha and omega. "The beginning and the end," interpreted Philo.

I pointed out a second image, a circle with a dot in the middle. "The circumference and the center," Philo inferred.

"It could be Christian. What to do we do next?" I asked.

"We could watch the tomb."

"It could be a long wait."

Outside, another beggar appeared. When I asked him if anyone frequented the tomb, he held out his hand. We found out that children, beggars like himself, and "visitors of the night" came here. When we pressed about whether a sect used the tomb, he shrugged his shoulders.

"Do any pass the night in there?" asked Philo.

"Ghosts guard it," said the man.

"An empty tomb guarded by spirits?" I wondered out loud.

Philo and I ended up sitting a distance from the tomb. We did not venture to sleep inside the rock-cut tomb itself. Since our source had mentioned the night, we alternated shifts. I watched in the day and Philo by night. For three days and two nights, we saw no visitors.

On the last day, however, the tomb had an unexpected visitor.

An older woman with long hair, dressed in a blue robe, came before the tomb, and sat silently for a time. When she stepped inside the tomb, I woke Philo. We rushed into the tomb, but she was nowhere to be found. We searched every empty slab and passage.

Philo said nothing.

"Maybe, it was a ghost," I said.

"I am no ghost," said the woman, stepping out of the shadows.

The voice was uncanny: How had she stayed hidden? Could she have disappeared and reappeared?

She waited as if this was her space and that an explanation was in order.

We told the truth, that we were searching for the Crucified One who was laid here many years ago.

Her answer surprised us. "Come and I will show you what you seek. But if its bones you look for, you will only find death."

Was it a trap? Where would she lead us? But we sense this was a woman of power, a prophetess, perhaps of the very cult we sought. Philo and I followed her in the dawning light.

The unnamed woman led us further away from the city and up a steep hill. We were amazed how fast she could move, despite her age. We were out of breath as we neared the top. There, we came upon a shattered Greek temple, where half columns stood. The sun shone through an entrance portal. Philo and I stepped through after the woman, and she was lost to sight.

We didn't see her vanish, for the brightness of the sun. But she was nowhere to be found among the ruins. We picked around, finding broken votive statues, pottery shards, and a few bones from animal sacrifices.

"Here," said Philo. He had come upon a side structure with an entrance leading down into the ground. "It looks like an underground temple, cut from an old tomb chamber."

As we stepped down, I sensed the structure was still in use. The light was dim in the forecourt and dimmer yet in the main structure. We bumped against benches and made out a cult statue.

I heard sudden noises and a scream. Someone was in my arms. It was Philo, bleeding. I drew my sword. Whoever it was had already withdrawn deeper into the chamber. I retreated, pulling Philo to the surface.

His face was peaceful, but a knife wound lay deep in his side. "A guardian of the precinct," he gasped. "I should have known."

Philo's life hung in the balance, and I didn't know what to do. I had bound his wound the best I could, staunching the flow of blood. But I could not risk carrying him. And to leave him on the hill with the murderer about seemed worse.

I could not believe what had happened. The mysterious woman disappearing into the night and us finding death. Why had she not warned us? Then I remembered her words not to look for bones, or we would find death.

Anger welled in me at this Christian cult. I raised my fist to the sky and asked repeatedly. *Why?*

In the end I thought to light a beacon fire, and soon soldiers arrived. Philo was taken on a litter back to the legionary's camp. They searched the premises and found the chamber led to a cave that narrowed into inaccessible passages. There was no sign of anyone. I asked the soldiers to look for bone deposits in the recesses. "The murderer is not to be found among bones," said the officer in charge.

"We're looking for other victims," I said, and I told of the emperor's orders.

The officer, knowing my connection to the centurion, indulged me. But they turned up no evidence. They even dug up under the main altar. Anything of value must be well hidden in a deep recess, I concluded.

The soldiers posted a guard, and I hastened to the palace to find out Philo's fate.

CHAPTER XX

ISLAND VISIONARY

We had gone to the burial tombs and found death waiting. It was bad luck going amid tombs. Outcasts, murderers, the insane favored these haunts and nosing about them finally caught up to us.

A wave of despair came over me. My closest associate was dying, and our mission unaccomplished. It was then that I miraculously ran into Kentra. On the road back to the Legionaries' camp, she was walking off to the side--it appeared aimlessly.

"You're still here!" I exclaimed.

"It's my home," she said.

"But the others have fled."

"There are a handful here in hiding," she revealed. I observed she was now of clear mind. For a moment I wondered if she was the woman Philo had been following. "Will you come with me," I asked. "Philo has been hurt."

Although Philo had been distant to her, she immediately went with me. We found him, pale and wan, going between consciousness and unconsciousness.

The doctor had wanted to blood let, but Philo would not allow it. He had weakened, and the doctor was beginning to proceed on his own. "He has already lost enough blood," I said, stopping the physician.

"Then there is nothing more to be done," he said.

We sat by Philo for hours. Kentra helped to keep him comfortable, and she prayed to her God. At points Philo became more conscious and spoke of a woman he saw, how she was like an angel. At one point he cried out, "The eagle-man is alive!" He had become delirious. Or was this a reference to the murderer? Philo calmed as if he had returned to an island of sanity. "I can see him," he said.

"Who?" I asked.

"The Eagle-man is one of the twelve."

"Did he do this to you?"

Philo didn't answer, his eyes following something, as if seeing a vision.

It started my mind whirling. What had led Philo to his near death? Was it the cult that protected their burial places? Yet, here was Kentra, a member of the cult, praying for his life. Were they a two-sided group––having a God who both killed and gave life?

I nodded off and woke in the morning. Kentra was still awake by his side. Philo had died. His face was at peace. Kentra and I both wept.

The question of where to bury Philo arose. The Jewish community had long fled. Burials were illegal. There were spots for Legionary soldiers, but I thought Philo would have preferred a different setting.

I asked Kentra if he could be buried among her people. They were a Jewish sect, after all.

With the help of Kentra's friends, her brother, and a handful of men and women, we buried Philo near to the tomb of the Missing One.

We had set out to find the Founder's bones, and we had only added more. He had conquered us and our search. Or was there another chance?

I took a last chance among the cult members. They would answer my questions now, I felt. In this way I found out the location of an aged man, the last of the twelve who lived on an island and saw visions.

My ship landed in the Greek city of Ephesus on the coast of Anatolia, under the shadow of Mount Pion. It was famous for being the home of philosophers and the cult of Cybele. When I arrived, however, an Imperial festival was in progress. Food from all parts of the world had arrived: exotic meats from Africa and spices from India. There was a general riot of celebration, which would only get worse during the period called the *License of the Gods.*

On the way to the Governor's palace, I passed the Temple of Artemis. The Greeks had renamed an ancient cult of Cybele's that had sent many pine-bodied Attises across the world. The temple's size made it one of the seven wonders of the world, and I was surprised to find it so quiet inside. Within the main hall stood a statue of the Goddess, her body laced with animals and covered with eggs. In the distance I saw a supplicant receiving an oracle. I waited. A bird flew through the temple and thunder sounded. The God's presence did not impress me. Philo had informed me about thunder machines hidden deep inside the temple and how birds were sent a flight for effect. The supplicant would pay more handsomely then.

The Governor was in no mood to discuss the Bone Cult, as it reminded him of a thorn in his side. "They refuse to recognize our gods and the emperor. They call his offerings the 'Meat of Idols.'"

When I asked about the Visionary, he told me the islands were infested with them. "The previous ruler exiled them to rocky islands where they bother people less."

"Which ones?"

"There are hundreds!" exclaimed the Governor. "Am I to keep track of where each madman lives?"

His patience had expired. "Are there any Christians here?" I asked, risking another question.

"A few in prison refusing to eat meat, but they talk less than they eat. Try their enemies, a rival cult from Pergamon."

I found them with a help of a local informant. They were not forthcoming, claiming to be a band of merchants. When I mentioned the Visionary, the Eagle man, their interest sparked. "Mad with visions. Intolerant. He called our town, the 'Throne of Satan,'" said one.

"Do you know where he is?"

"Are you one of them?"

"No, I am a Roman. They are under investigation," I said, hoping to gain more information.

"He should not be hard to find. The government has exiled him to Patmos."

"I have heard they believe there is power in bones."

"Only the spirit is real," said the man, which showed he belonged to a different cult. "And the one they say who died is the 'Laughing God.' He never suffered; a real God does not feel pain."

Ignoring this theological difference, I said, "They say his bones are missing. Do you know where they are?"

"You're a seeker of bones?" asked the man, looking at me askance. "Go ask the Eagle-man."

Taking a small sailing vessel, I headed to the island of Patmos. I arrived to silence and a feeling of isolation among a few winged gulls. As I tracked across rocky wastes, lizards shot under the stones as I passed. On a projection on the far seaside, I found him.

I asked his name, and he answered John. His face was ancient but bore signs of thought and kindness.

"Are you one of the twelve?"

"Do I disturb the emperor even here?" The trace of anger appeared for only a moment, before laughter came to his eyes and put me at ease. I sat down.

"The emperor is bothered," I admitted. I told about the prophecy and the phoenix. "We have found only bones until now."

"No wonder," he said. "The Dragon has swallowed them. But the bones of the Lamb he could not digest, and he has spewed them back out. These bones have taken shape again, and so they still fight."

"It is hard to kill twice," I admitted.

The man nodded his head. There was a long silence. I knew for sure he was one of the twelve. Should I bring him back to Rome, to keep his bones from littering this Rocky isle. If he were the last of the twelve, the Phoenix would rise at his death, according to the prophecy. But at this great age, he could die anytime. The stress of a trip and imprisonment would only hasten his death. For a moment, the absurdity overwhelmed me—an old man having visions on an isolated rock was a threat to Rome.

"The Missing One," I said. "Where have they hidden him?"

"The child is hidden. The Eagle has carried them off, the babe and his mother. I have seen them in the desert."

The apostle was obviously recounting a vision, and I didn't know what to make of it. Then the seer began to walk further up the mountain, moving surprisingly fast for his age. I followed. A cloud circled the mountaintop, which suddenly came to view, topped with snow. At the very top, a clear crystal vein broke through. On it lay ritual implements, including a cup with serpentine designs. I wondered if he performed in private the ritual cannibalism of their leader.

The seer entered into a light trance, his hands mildly trembling, his face radiant. Gradually, the mist cleared on one side of the mountain. Suddenly you could see for miles, to the distant coast.

Something strange happened next. A sea eagle suddenly landed on the far side of the rock, a large snake in its mouth. This would hardly seem remarkable, but events did not stop there. The eagle looked up at us instead of feasting on the snake. It was a poisonous viper, still living, but it did not bite the eagle.

What happened next is only the more fantastic, and perhaps only possible because of the fog, the presence of the seer, and the unusual juxtaposition of snake and eagle. The eagle loosed the snake; it coiled up, as if to strike. I called out in warning, but the snake rubbed its head against the rock. Then it raised its head, and out of its gaping mouth, a figure emerged. I thought it might regurgitate bones, but an infant child with upraised arms appeared.

Only for a moment, and it vanished. The eagle flew off, leaving only the snake's skin on the rock. I picked it up, its scales shimmering like a rainbow. My mind was in a daze, wondering what I had seen.

The aged seer looked abnormally still and white. Had he died? Yes ... and I realized I had witnessed the moment of the rising Phoenix. It was not a literal Phoenix....

The grass rustled and something slithered nearby. I had forgotten about the living viper. I ran down the mountain.

At the bottom, I glanced back up at the top. The clouds had cleared, and I saw something flashing. Then from the sea, a boat was arriving....

EPILOG

The librarian abruptly closed the scroll and stated, "Here the writing ends."

"What?" asked Constantine. "Nothing more? What happened to our investigator?"

"He drops out of history."

"Did he reach Rome?"

"I have checked the official records, but there is no further mention of him."

"It sounds like foul play. What do you think Eusebius?"

The manuscript ends at a critical moment. Anything could have happened. But I am intrigued by the vision at the end. *What emerged from the snake? Was it good or evil?*

"I doubt that the vision killed our investigator," said the librarian.

"Killed?" said Helena, the wife of Constantine.

"A right arm man of the emperor just doesn't drop out of history," said the librarian. "Something happened."

"If he was murdered, who did it?" asked Helena. "Certainly, not the Christians."

"They have the most obvious motive," said the librarian. "After all, the investigator was trying to discredit them. Perhaps they thought he was an assassin."

"The boat at the end," said the emperor, "could have been the followers of John. When they discovered their leader dead and a Roman agent on the island, they killed him."

"But the followers of John taught love as a command. It would more likely the act of a violent sect, like the one who killed Philo," said Eusebius.

"There is no motive for the other sects," said the emperor.

"Maybe the anti-John sect murdered the official, to blame the Christians," Eusebius argued.

"There would have been an investigation," said the librarian. "Yet we hear nothing."

"Perhaps he went mad," said Lactantius, the poet. "He had gone the lengths of the earth, looking for the twelve, only to find bones. When he finally finds a live one, he too dies before his eyes, and after a vision which he could only interpret as the birth of the Phoenix and failure of his mission. He commits suicide."

"But the tale, he had time to write the tale, and nearly finish it. How could he have gone mad? He must have survived for some time," reasoned the librarian.

"Perhaps it was a sorcerer's hand from early on?" said Lactantius.

"You're grasping at straws," said Helena. "We have all failed to look at the most obvious. The main suspect is the emperor himself. We don't hear of the investigator's arrival in Rome or his disappearance in Greece because the emperor himself had him disposed. Obviously, it would be erased from official annals."

"A plausible theory," said Constantine. "The boat then would be the emperor's henchmen. The investigator had time to finish his tale up to a point. He hid the scroll and later, the followers of John found and preserved it."

"But would the emperor kill his own man?" asked Eusebius. "Do we have enough motive, more than he was not successful in this one mission?

"We do not have all the documents," allowed the librarian. "We know he sent letters to the emperor, expressing his doubts, maybe his sympathies. The emperor, in his fears, felt that his own man was betraying him, and sent his men to assassinate him."

"Perhaps the final vision converted him to the faith," said Helena.

"That goes beyond the proofs we have!" countered the librarian.

"What do you think Eusebius?" asked the emperor.

"We are left with a mystery. We don't know whether he converted, Yet why else would he have written in such profuse detail, if was not intrigued, at least half-way believed."

"He searched and was true to his search," agreed Helena. "His mission was to disprove the faith, yet he could not. He sent back no lies. He could have sent any old bones and claimed to have found the Missing One, but he didn't. He started to wonder if it was true...."

"It is like the dream he had in the beginning," said Lactantius. "The phoenix killed him. He searched to his death. He was a martyr in finding the truth."

"The patron saint of detectives!" announced the emperor. "We should find his bones, and give them proper burial, and build a church over them."

"No," said Eusebius. I think there is a more fitting tribute. "Have you not dreamed of gathering the bones of the twelve with yourself in a central coffin? You had dismissed this as a wild fantasy, but you are the phoenix from the oracle! *From the bones of twelve, a Phoenix shall rise that will rule Rome.* You are the one to rise and rule the New Rome in the Christian name! The Investigator was trying to stop you, but he failed."

"The Investigator has inspired me," said Constantine. "This day will begin the great search to find the bones of the twelve. Then we will build a church over them."

"The Church of the Twelve Apostles," named Eusebius.

"I too will start a search for the Missing One––not his bones, but for the remains of his cross," Helena decided.

"I have been inspired too," said Eusebius. "If an investigator can faithfully write this much, I will begin my history of the church."

"And I will write a poem," said Lactantius, "and call it the *Phoenix*!"

"What about you?" asked the emperor to the aged fossores. "You have remained silent all this time, yet but for you, this story would have been lost."

"I will return to the catacombs and dig around some more," said the fossores. "Who knows what one will find."

The End

Don't miss out!

Visit the website below and you can sign up to receive emails whenever Michael A. Susko publishes a new book. There's no charge and no obligation.

https://books2read.com/r/B-A-GJLJ-YQARB

BOOKS2READ

Connecting independent readers to independent writers.

Did you love *Twelve Suspects*? Then you should read *Guard of the Dead*[1] by Michael A. Susko!

[2]

These stories are inspired by persons who appear in the Gospels for only a few sentences. It imagines the drama of their encounter with a founder of a world religion at the time of the Roman Empire. Internal worlds are opened up, including a soldier who guards the dead, a madman who lives among tombs, a woman who battles demons, and Levianthan, a storm which would take the founder's life. What surprises us more than 2,000 years later is how much heart and fierce love is present in the lives of these characters.

Read more at https://www.allroneofus.com/.

---

1. https://books2read.com/u/3JZpDg

2. https://books2read.com/u/3JZpDg

Also by Michael A. Susko

A Couple Through Time
Down Below and the Archon's Castle
Up Above and the Runaway
Across the Gulf and Journey Into Un-Time
On the Bay and a Child Found
In the Wild and Do One Wild Thing
On the Mountain and Two Are Missing
To the Beginning and Journey Through Here

Archetypal Worlds
Alwon in Another World: An Archetypal Voyage
Line On the Wall
The Alien's Gift
The Gold People
Spider Woman and the Timeroc
Quill Ears & the Other Earth
Darkwood and Dual with the Shadow Side
Giant Under the Mountain

Haikus and Photos

Flowers and Haikus
Haikus and Photos: Guatemalan Highlands
Haikus and Photos: Water Birds and Reflections
Haikus and Photos: Seasons of New River
Haikus and Photos: Yosemite Wilderness
Haikus and Photos: California Coast
Haikus and Photos: Canadian Rockies
Haikus and Photos: Hawaii's Exotic Landscapes
Haikus and Photos: Vienna, People with Buildings and Art
Haikus and Photos: Slovakian Castles and Hamlets
Haikus and Photos: Berlin, Light and Dark
Haikus and Photos: New Orleans, City of Immigrants
Haikus and Photos: Antietam Wind and Spirits
Haikus & Photos: Plant Abstractions
Haikus and Photos: Appalachian Beauty
Haikus and Photos: Urban Farm in Sandtown
Haikus and Photos: New York Heights and Ground
Haikus & Photos: Santa Fe Fractal-Pueblo Spirtuality
Haikus and Photos: Monticello's Double Vision

Little Lion
The Lion and the Chameleon
The Elephant and the Chameleons

Nature Haikus & Photos
Haikus and Photos: Butterflies and Flowers
Haikus and Photos: A Cardinal's Life
Haikus and Photos: Two Racoons at Play
Haikus and Photos: Hawaiian Green Sea Turtle
Haikus and Photos: Irises in the Rain

Child of the Elements
The Firekeeper
Ten Pulses of Evolution & the Surprising Nature of Evolutionary
Time
Up Above and Down Below
Life's Dynamic Vulnerability: A Paradigm Shift in Biology
Alien Ally
The Generation of Life: Imagery, Ritual and Experiences in Deep
Caves
Twelve Suspects
2084: Clash of the Cults
Guard of the Dead
The Imagination Being
Ten Traits of Empire that Every Person Should Know
Aging and Renewal: Living the Full Life
The Meaning, Beauty & Mystery of Dreams: Seven Guidelines and
Seven Tools for Listening
A Rosetta Key for History: The Generational Pattern of Time

Watch for more at https://www.allroneofus.com/.

About the Author

The author, who holds degrees in Philosophy and Counseling Psychology, has an interest in combining the arts and sciences. He helped found a progressive elementary school, which featured science and arts integration. His published work in nonfiction and fiction seeks to provide a coherent vision of the world that is continually becoming.

Read more at https://www.allroneofus.com/.